$9⁹²

D1067797

MISS MINERVA
AND WILLIAM GREEN HILL

• TENNESSEANA EDITIONS •

Miss Minerva

AND WILLIAM GREEN HILL

By Frances Boyd Calhoun

Illustrated by Angus Macdonall

A FACSIMILE EDITION

WITH AN INTRODUCTION BY

Robert Drake

THE UNIVERSITY OF TENNESSEE PRESS

TENNESSEANA EDITIONS

Nathalia Wright, General Editor

**Library of Congress Cataloging in
Publication Data**

Calhoun, Frances Boyd, 1867–1909.
  Miss Minerva and William Green Hill.

  Reprint of the 1911 ed. published by Reilly
& Britton Co., Chicago; with new introd.
  I. Title
PZ3.C1285Mi17   [PS3505.A376]
813'.5'2   75-20498
ISBN 0-87049-182-2

CONTENTS

INTRODUCTION TO THE
NEW EDITION

FRANCES BOYD CALHOUN never knew her own
success. Having published her one masterpiece,
Miss Minerva and William Green Hill, on
February 6, 1909, she died on June 8 of that
same year and consequently never learned of
the affection and esteem in which the book
came to be held by successive generations of
readers, the more than fifty printings through
which the work passed, nor its subsequent
extension into a sequel, *Billy and the Major*
(1918), by Emma Speed Sampson (1868-
1947), then its expansion into a series of nearly
a dozen volumes, also by Mrs. Sampson.

Though *Miss Minerva and William Green
Hill* is laid in Covington, Tennessee, an actual
West Tennessee town nearly forty miles above
Memphis, and hardly ever strays from that lo-
cale and though Mrs. Calhoun, in a letter to
her publishers, described herself as "a Southerner of Southerners," the book could not be
called "regional" in any except the broadest
and most comprehensive sense. Surely, the
Southern machinery is there, the speech, the
manners of both white and black—and presented in such fashion as might cause the

hackles of contemporary zealots or racists of whatever persuasion to rise, so faithfully and truly is it rendered. But Mrs. Calhoun did not falsify the life she knew, nor did she try to dress it up as a commodity for export, as is the way with cheap local color artists. She looked at this life steadily and recorded it faithfully; and she was not grinding an ax for racism, the social and political *status quo*, or any particular ideology.

If she seems to condescend to Negroes, she is not blind to the faults of the whites; indeed, she might even be taken as implying some sort of racial double standard—one much more exacting on the whites than on their darker brethren. Uncle Tomism? Perhaps so, if you like. But such was the context in which Mrs. Calhoun wrote—a white man's world but one made possible all along the way by the endeavors and attitudes of Negroes—and she could not have modified it without being false to it and ultimately to her art. (Indeed, the disparity between the races later emerges as an important thematic consideration—and one not always flattering to the white man.)

But race is not her subject here: all Mrs. Calhoun cared about, it would seem, was telling the truth about a boy's growing up in a particular world (which just happens, in this case, to be West Tennessee) and his crucial and overriding determination to frustrate the powerful but well-meant zeal of his old-maid aunt to root out, smooth down, and deodorize all his untrammeled boyishness and supplant it with a sort of feminine submissiveness and grace. (When the orphan boy first comes to live with her, she resolves to bring him up as if he were a girl!) In short, she wants to turn him into a sissy. And this is a very old story indeed and goes on—and has done so—all the time, in Covington, Tennessee, New York City, Timbuktu, or anywhere else.

The book was published in Chicago, too, though this may have been due as much to the dearth of publishing facilities in the South as to the book's wider, non-regional appeal. But, as indicated in "The Publishers' Story of *Miss Minerva and William Green Hill*," which was appended to later editions of the work (a reprint is included in this current edition), what caught the eye of Messrs. Reilly and Britton (later Reilly and Lee, which ultimately became associated with the Henry Regnery Company) was more than geography and quaint folkways, manners and morals; it was the "surprise and delight" of discovering the work of an author who "gave promise of adding so much to the store of human happiness." This has been the experience of several generations of readers not only in the South but all over the country—readers who would not hesitate to apply the adjective *beloved* to the book, signifying the very real affection they feel for this celebration of the joys of childhood—joys coupled with some sadness, especially for us, the readers, who know, as the children do not as yet fully comprehend, that some day they too will have to grow up and turn, if not into joy-killing Miss Minervas, at least into "sivilized" adults (Huck Finn's spelling, remember).

This may be as good a place as any to deal with the remark once made by a visiting professor of English from Italy to whom I had lent my treasured copy of the book. He read it with considerable interest, I gather; but his sole comment on the work, as I recall, was: "That woman certainly knows her Mark Twain." I remember now how angry his remark made me. And then I asked myself what else you could expect from an English teacher (whether Italian or otherwise), trained as he was to look for *influences* and other abstract relationships and considerations at every turn. And all of it in books too. What did he know about life anyhow? Surely, Mrs. Calhoun was in Mark Twain's debt in that she and all other American writers (Ring Lardner and Sherwood Anderson, for example) who came after him learned from him something about the literary uses of colloquial, even vulgar or substandard language. (Surely, Hemingway had something like this in mind—among other things—when he observed, in *Green Hills of Africa*, that all modern American literature comes from a book called *Huckleberry Finn*.) But Mark Twain never gave Mrs. Calhoun what she was born with: a good ear and a good eye for the spoken words and characteristic actions of

her place, her region, and her people. She knew
instinctively, I should think, how character is
revealed, indeed often betrayed, in word and
action: in this sense, she had been preparing
all her life to write her book. She had, like all
good writers, most surely done a lot of listening, a lot of looking; but consciously, she was
not playing the sedulous ape to anyone. And
nearly anybody but an English professor would
automatically know better. Like Mark Twain,
Mrs. Calhoun grew up in a culture which placed
a high value on the spoken word, the told tale,
and the traditional strategies employed there-
in. But it would be misguided to see him as
wielding some sort of influence over her. He
merely pointed the way, most of which she
had already found out for herself.

The bare facts of Mrs. Calhoun's life are
briefly related. Born Frances Boyd in Mecklenburg County, Virginia, on December 25, 1867,
she later lived for about two years in Warrenton, North Carolina, before moving to Tennessee in 1880. She graduated from the Tipton
Female Seminary in Covington in 1885. Later,
she assisted her father in editing a local newspaper, occasionally publishing poetry there
and in one of the Memphis papers, and taught
for seven years in the primary grades of the
Covington city school. In 1903, she married
George Barret Calhoun, who died a year later.
Mrs. Calhoun herself survived him by only five
years. Nearly all pertinent information about
her (one infers that she cherished her privacy,

by the way) is contained in "The Publishers' Story" cited earlier, though some Covington-ians who knew her are still alive and have been kind enough to pass on some of their memories of her to me.

Nearly all the characters in the book are based on real-life originals; Mrs. Edwin H. Brown, the Lina Hamilton of the book, has written me that, though Mrs. Calhoun did not, as I had erroneously supposed, teach her and the other principal characters (William Green Hill, Jimmy Garner, and Frances Black—all real children) in the Covington school, she knew their parents well and, I assume, thought it would be amusing to try putting their children into a book. Furthermore, Mrs. Brown, in an interview, observed that the four principals were not all the same age (she was the oldest) and not such inseparable companions as the book suggests. Another Covington informant, Mrs. Sam C. Shelton, has written me that Mrs. Calhoun (the perennial old-maid schoolteach-er?) may have fancied herself in the role of Miss Minerva and perhaps her husband as the Major, Miss Minerva's persistent suitor. Mrs. Shelton also asserts the factuality of much of the book. All the pranks, for example, were really committed, she says, but by different children, not even necessarily by characters in the book. Many of the names used were the names of real people. But both Mrs. Shelton and Mrs. Brown have confirmed, in interviews, that Mrs. Calhoun took the raw material of "fact" and shaped it into the *form* of fiction: like any good fiction writer, she was not tied to reporting or recording but rather to constructing and creating. Thus she contrived situations more dramatic than historic, all for the sake of the story. Whatever the case, it does seem logical to infer that Mrs. Calhoun's years in the classroom, as well as her native endowment of wit and humor (Mrs. Shelton and Mrs. Brown seem to agree that Mrs. Calhoun was a natural storyteller), made her perceive all the more sharply the dramatic possibilities inherent in the collision between the world of these children and that of the adults.

For that is what the book is basically about. William Green Hill is at war with the prim and proper Miss Minerva, who is his aunt; and the three other comrades join him in the warfare, not only against Miss Minerva but also against all adults, who are mostly all Miss Minervas writ less, with two signal exceptions—the Major, Miss Minerva's faithful but hitherto unsuccessful suitor, and Sam Lamb, the Negro employee of the livery stable. This Confederate veteran (Joseph is all the name given him except for Billy's "Major Minerva"), who reputedly has fought both Indians and Yankees and had his big toe shot off in the process, and the Negro bus driver conspire with the four children, wittingly or not, to counteract the efforts of the adult world to ignore the precious blessings of free and unlimited childhood and impose all too soon the inevitable yoke, the shades of the prison house, upon their high spirits and vital joys.

And these two exceptions may not be without significance. The Major, who is only too glad to call William "Billy," as he prefers, seems to represent the masculine principle pure and simple. Indeed, he incarnates the "pants" principle itself. We are told by Jimmy, as he instructs Billy in the ways of his new home at the beginning of the book, that "Miss Minerva she just turns up her nose at anything that wears pants." But his—and Billy's—triumph is complete at the book's end when Miss Minerva, at the insistence of her impetuous and long-suffering lover, agrees to marry him the very next day: "No, not next Sunday or Monday or Tuesday. We will be married tomorrow," he asserts. Thus he can help her "make a fine, manly boy out of that nephew of yours." The delighted Billy only wants to know whether his aunt is going to marry the Major "Pants an' all."

The case of Sam Lamb may be somewhat different. (He too existed "for real.") Of course, he is a male also and presumably committed to helping Billy and the other children prevent the threatened imposition of the feminine, genteel-making, ultimately emasculating principle on their lives. (Here men and children seem in league against the women.) But also he is a *black* man and as such may be seen as a person from outside the white com-

munity invoking sanctions against the femi-
nizing principle, sanctions which the white
community may ignore to its ultimate detri-
ment, even peril. So perhaps another aspect
of the racial double standard—an inverted aspect possibly—may once more be seen at
work in the book: black knows more than
white about relations between children and
adults, just as, earlier, men seem to know
more than women, children sometimes more
than adults. Thus a continual paradox is spun
out on something like the theme of the first
shall be last and the last, first.

For this is the war which is fought out during
the whole course of the book—the war between adults and children. And there are no
holds barred here. We are accustomed, in a
good deal of modern fiction, to seeing children
distressed and oppressed—or at least thinking
that they are. Many of them seem like crazy,
mixed-up kids, more sinned against than sin-
ning perhaps, many of them searching for the
elusive happiness that seems to lie just beyond
their grasp and forever, like Holden Caulfield,
looking out at the "phony" world they never
made, by which they feel somehow betrayed.
But there is none of that here, and this we see
more and more as the plot unfolds. So it is at
this point that some rehearsal of the novel's
story seems in order.

Miss Minerva and William Green Hill is
the story of a six-year-old orphan, William

Green Hill, who comes to live with his Aunt
Minerva in Covington, Tennessee. (The real
William Green Hill, by the way, was not an
orphan; he was also a first cousin of the book's
Jimmy Garner. But again, Mrs. Calhoun knew
what she was about, for the purposes of fiction.) Billy, as he insists on being called, much
to the dismay of his aunt, has lived all his life
on a big plantation, associating only with Negroes, especially Wilkes Booth Lincoln, whom
he calls his "twin" because they were born on
the same day, "only I's borned to my mamma
an' he's borned to his'n." Miss Minerva, who
appears as the conventionally refined and genteel maiden lady of the South, is truly, as the
title of the first chapter tells us, a scandalized
virgin when she first confronts all the untamed
boyishness of her nephew. She really had not
wanted him, anyhow—this child of the younger
sister, whose runaway marriage had provoked
Miss Minerva's displeasure. But now both the
sister and the "wild, reckless, dissipated
brother-in-law" are dead; and the boy has
been sent to her. But a way out of her dilemma
occurs to Miss Minerva: she resolves that,
though Billy is not a girl, she will rear him
just as if he were and he will grow up to be "a
model young man, a splendid and wonderful
piece of mechanism, a fine, practical, machine-like individual, moral, upright, religious." Later on, he will be educated for the
ministry. The stage is thus set for the novel's
central conflict; and the remainder of the book

is hilariously concerned with the frustration of her grand design by Billy, the Major, and their allies.

But the real joy of the book is Billy and his playmates: Jimmy Garner, "the bad little boy who lives next door," Frances Black, and Lina Hamilton. These children, who all, as has been previously noted, were based on real models (Jimmy, really Sanford, Garner and Frances Black are now dead, and William Green Hill himself, according to a newspaper clipping of May 4, 1964, met a somewhat sad and sordid end—he was found dead in destitute circumstances in a railway freight car), display a realism in their dealings with the adult, civilized world which makes our modern child-heroes—or, more properly, child-victims—look like what they really are: scandalized virgins, who thought, until their inevitable and sometimes rude awakening, that the world was run on mathematical principles of liberty and justice for all. There is, significantly, never any questioning, on the part of these four children, of the *right* of adults to discipline them. It is an open and fair fight, though, in which the rights of each side are explicitly defined in a way that is almost impossible in a society which has come to believe more and more that orders and degrees jar not with liberty, a society which can, moreover, all too easily forgive in the child what it would be very quick to condemn in the adult. Notice what happens when the four children are detected in the act of playing Indian (with a treasured Navaho blanket and a beautiful afghan) by "our mammas and Miss Minerva," who have all been to a meeting of the Ladies' Aid Society.

> "'T ain't no use to run," advised Jimmy. "They're too close and done already see us. We boun' to get what's coming to us anyway, so you might jus' as well make 'em think you ain't afraid of 'em. Grown folks got to all time think little boys and girls 'r' skeered of 'em, anyhow."

And again, when the children climb a ladder to get up on Miss Minerva's newly painted roof,

> "Don't we have fun?" cried a jubilant Frances.
> "Yes," answered Jimmy; "if grown folks don't all time be watching you and sticking theirselfs in your way."
> "If people would let us alone," remarked Lina, "we could enjoy ourselves every day."
> "But grown folks got to be so pertic'lar with you all time," cried Jimmy, "they don't never want us to play together."

These child-heroes, then, have much more in common with that arch-antagonist of the artificially civilized, Huckleberry Finn, and with Saki's inexorably realistic and unregenerate little demons than they do with an engaging but confused young boy like Mr. Salinger's Holden Caulfield, who can accept neither adults nor himself. For them, all is fair in their ceaseless war on adult decorum; but they never question the right of such decorum to exist, any more than they question the necessity of mammas and papas. It is only artificial decorum and "refinement" that really nettles them, as it does Huckleberry Finn. Is it possible, then, that in their infant wisdom they know it is not long until sheer morning gladness must give way to the sober thoughts of man's mortality and that they must take the harmless follies of the time now? Indeed, the stirrings toward decorum are evident in Lina, who is the most "adult" of the children and who often sides with the supremely realistic Billy against the untamed Frances and Jimmy. Her leanings are manifest when she refuses to let Jimmy be "Setting Bull" in the Indian game.

"You can't be named 'Bull,' Jimmy," reproved Lina, "it is n't genteel to say 'bull' before people."

"Yes, I am too," he contended. "Setting Bull 's the biggest chief they is and I'm going to be name' him."

"Well, I am not going to play then," said Lina primly, "my mother wants me to be genteel, and 'bull' is not genteel."

"I tell you what, Jimmy," proposed Frances, "you be name' 'Setting Cow.' 'Cow' is genteel 'cause folks milk 'em."

"Naw, I ain't going to be name' no cow, neither," retorted the little Indian, "you all time trying to 'suade somebody to be name' 'Setting Cow.'"

"He can't be name' a cow,"—Billy now entered into the discussion—"'cause he ain't no girl. Why don' you be name' 'Settin' Steer'? Is 'steer' genteel, Lina?" he anxiously inquired.

"Yes, he can be named 'Sitting Steer,'" she granted. Jimmy agreeing to the compromise, peace was once more restored.

Also, Lina wants to be a "lady" when she grows up. This is in sharp contrast to Frances, who is still unregenerate.

"I'm glad I am going to be a young lady when I grow up," Lina declared, "I would n't be a gentleman for anything. I'm going to wear pretty clothes and be beautiful and be a belle like mother was, and have lots of lovers kneel at my feet on one knee and play the guitar with the other—"

"How they goin' to play the guitar with they other knee?" asked the practical Billy.

"And sing 'Call Me Thy Own,'" she continued, ignoring his interruption. "Father got on his knees to mother thirty-seven-and-a-half times before she'd say, 'I will.'"

"Look like he 'd 'a' wore his breeches out," said Billy.

"I don't want to be a lady," declared Frances; "they can't ever ride straddle nor climb a tree, and they got to squinch up their waists and toes. I wish I could kiss my elbow right now and turn to a boy."

These two conversations raise, almost explicitly, the conflict between male and female principles which permeates the book. And doubtless, readers and critics of a Freudian persuasion would make a great deal of them: the male as the life-fulfiller and the female, at least in this case, as the castrator or life-betrayer. But perhaps it is the wrong kind of femininity which is the villain here, not the principle itself. The real villain of the piece, all along, seems "objective," "rational," artificializing adulthood, of whatever gender. Certainly (again here's the racial irony), Billy's memories of the Negro women such as Aunt

Cindy and Peruny Pearline back on the plantation are warmly affectionate. But Lina and Frances, we feel, will never turn into rigidly unrealistic Miss Minervas or world-weary sophisticates because they are aware that reality is too complex and too "deep" to be simplified by either gentility or science (are gentility and science different sides of the same coin?) and too exciting ever to become dull.

This brings us to one of the most striking characteristics of these children—their wholehearted acceptance of myth as reality. Being brought up in the fundamentalist South, they are intimately, if not always accurately, acquainted with Bible figures and events and see nothing contradictory or incredible in talking about God as if He lived next door.

"Ain't God a nice, good old man," remarked Billy, after they had swung in silence for a while, with an evident desire to make talk.

"That He is," replied Jimmy, enthusiastically. "He 's 'bout the forgivingest person ever was. I just could n't get 'long at all 'thout Him. It don't make no differ'nce what you do or how many times you run off, all you got to do is just ask God to forgive you and tell him you 're sorry and ain't going to do so no more, that night when you say your prayers, and it's all right with God. S'posing He was one of these wants-his-own-way kind o' mans, He could make Hi'self the troublesomest person ever was, and little boys could n't do nothing a tall. I sure think a heap of God. He ain't never give me the worst of it yet."

"I wonder what He looks like," mused Billy.

"I s'pec' He just looks like the three-headed giant in Jack the Giant-Killer," explained Jimmy, "'cause He's got three heads and one body. His heads are name' Papa, Son, and Holy Ghost, and His body is just name' plain God. . . ."

This conversation displays the same respectfully familiar piety that we see in the Negro renderings of Bible stories by Roark Bradford, who, by the way, grew up in the next county to Mrs. Calhoun's Covington.

The man in the land of Uz, who might have had a few things to say to our disenchanted child-victims of today, is also well known to the children.

". . . He's in the Bible and he sold his birthmark for a mess of potatoes and—"

"You never can get anything right, Jimmy," interrupted Lina; "that was Esau and it was not his birthmark, it was his birthstone; and he sold his birthstone for a mess of potash."

"Yas," agreed Frances; "'he saw Esau kissing Kate and Esau had to sell him his birthstone to keep his mouth shut."

"Mother read me all about Job," continued Lina; "he was afflicted with boils and his wife knit him a Job's comforter to wrap around him, and he—"

"And he sat under a 'tato vine," put in Frances eagerly, "what God grew to keep the sun off o' his boils and—"

"That was Jonah," said Lina, "and it wasn't a potato vine; it was—"

"No, 't was n't Jonah neither' Jonah is inside of a whale's bel—"

"Frances!"

"Stommick," Frances corrected herself, "and a

whale swallow him, and how 's he going to sit under a pumpkin vine when he's inside of a whale?"

"It was not a pumpkin vine, it—"

"And I'd jus' like to see a man inside of a whale
a-setting under a morning-glory vine."

"The whale vomicked him up," said Jimmy.

And Elisha, who perhaps did not appreciate
juvenile impertinence—call it lack of inhibi-
tion or just plain bad manners—is very real
also, as we learn when Frances makes her
contribution to an afternoon of story-telling.

"Once there 's a man named Mr. Elisha, and he
had a friend named Mr. Elijah, so his mantelpiece
fell on top of his head and make him perfectly
bald; he has n't got a single hair and he has n't got
any money, 'cause mama read me 'bout he rented
his garments, which is clo'es, 'cause he did n't have
none at all what belong to him. I s'pec' he just
rented him a shirt and a pair of breeches and wore
'em next to his hide 'thout no undershirt at all. He
was drea'ful poor and had a miser'able time and
old mean Mr. Per'dventure took him up on a high
mountain and left him, so when he come down
some bad little childern say, 'Go, 'long back, bald
head!' and they make pock-mocks on him. Seems
like everybody treat him bad, so he cuss 'em, so I
never see anybody with a bald head 'thout I run,
'cause I don't want to get cussed. So two Teddy
bears come out of the woods and ate up forty-two
hunderd of 'em."

"Why Frances," reproved Lina, "you always get
things wrong. I don't believe they ate up that
many children."

"Yes, they did too," championed Jimmy, "'cause
it 's in the Bible and Miss Cecilia 'splained all 'bout
it to me, and she's our Sunday-School teacher and

> 'bout the bullyest 'splainer they is. Them Teddy
> bears ate up 'bout a million chillens, which is all
> the little boys and girls two Teddy bears can hold
> at a time."

What these children have, then, is something
very precious indeed. It is a knowledge, which
they of course do not and cannot articulate,
that myth (a myth, of course, shared by the
whole society) is "real," perhaps of ultimate
importance in giving the sanctions for action
in the everyday world, the world which is so
scandalizing to Miss Minerva and the other
virgins who try to abstract from reality the
"genteel" or the "factual"—or whatever aspect they happen to fancy—and pretend that
the rest of it does not exist.

In the end, however, Miss Minerva's cam-
paign to "civilize" Billy is defeated—just as
surely as the Widow Douglas' and Aunt Sally
Phelps' like endeavors are with Huck in
Huckleberry Finn—and she realizes, finally,
how much she has come to love him as he
really is, pants and all. When Billy and Jimmy
run off on a Negro railroad excursion to Memphis and the adults are distracted with worry
over their whereabouts, Miss Minerva defends
Billy against Mrs. Garner's accusation that it
was he who had led Jimmy astray.

> Miss Minerva's face blazed with indignation.
> "William's fault indeed!" she answered back.
> "There never was a sweeter child than William;"
> for the lonely woman knew the truth at last. At the
> thought that her little nephew might be hurt, a

long forgotten tenderness stirred her bosom and
she realized for the first time how the child had
grown into her life.

When the telegram arrives saying that the
boys have been found (appropriately enough
by Sam Lamb), the Major, who has come to
console Miss Minerva in her trial, sees his advantage and declares that they will be married the very next day so that he can help her
make "a fine, manly boy" out of Billy, who, he
says, is simply "full of natural animal spirits
and has to find some outlet for them." Miss
Minerva at first demurs; but the Major, his
newly found boldness adding determination to
his suit, prevails.

> "To-morrow! To-morrow! To-morrow!" cried the
> Major, happy as a schoolboy.
> "Next Sunday night after church," pleaded Miss
> Minerva.
> "No, not next Sunday or Monday or Tuesday.
> We will be married to-morrow," declared the dic-
> tatorial Confederate veteran.
> Billy's aunt succumbed.
> "Oh, Joseph," she said with almost a simper,
> "you are so masterful."

So Miss Minerva's conversion is complete,
and the realism of Billy and the Major is tri-
umphant. It is a victory for the truth of total
reality and full-bodied myth over the half-
truths of artificial gentility and emasculating
decorum. Childhood wins too, and straight
dealing and forthright talk come out ahead.
Men, to some extent, win over women: the
strong-minded war goddess, with whom Miss

Minerva's name identifies her, must submit to a superior power. And blacks, to a degree, triumph over whites. Deadening convention and moribund custom are exploded, while genuine tradition and life-giving order are vindicated. But it's all a victory for life over death, not an impertinent revolution or an impudent gesture. Yes, adulthood must come, Mrs. Calhoun implies; but it need not be a deadener and is not therefore necessarily an evil. Life and death are the fundamental issues here, and children need not die when they become grownups. So the book abides as a kind of perpetual celebration of the freshness, the directness, the sheer wonderful joy of childhood—but a joy like Wordsworth's, which, though bound to grow soberer as the years advance, need not ultimately pass away.

It was understandable if somewhat unfortunate that this delightful book should be followed with a sequel, then extended into a series (it was the time of the series too). The publishers and Mrs. Sampson (who lived in Richmond, Virginia) all knew a good thing when they saw it and were reluctant not to take the gifts the gods had provided. But, on the whole, Mrs. Sampson's series, which includes, besides *Billy and the Major,* such titles as *Miss Minerva's Baby* (1920), *Miss Minerva on the Old Plantation* (1923), and *Miss Minerva Broadcasts Billy* (1925), degenerates into mawkishness and sentimentality, as well as self-conscious coyness and

cuteness. There is no irony to qualify the
sweetness and no real steel to provide the
backbone for the novels: it's just some more
winsome didoes reported about the wee folk
in Covington, Tennessee, and ultimately
doesn't *mean* anything. And the fate which
overtakes Miss Minerva here is a very cruel
one indeed. Admittedly, she needs to be
chastened and subdued but surely not de-
stroyed as a character by being turned into
someone else. Yes, we're prepared to see her
married to the Major and humanized at his
and Billy's hands. But Mrs. Sampson makes
her have a baby (named Josephine) and become maternal and doting, which is really too
much. She is no longer "our" Miss Minerva
but a simpering stranger who Billy fancies re-
sembles his own mother (who died at his
birth) when he sees her with her own baby for
the first time. Such a "conversion" is unrealistic and incredible, and the work suffers ac-
cordingly.

  Mrs. Sampson's ear was by no means so
good as Mrs. Calhoun's either, and her use of
colloquial diction and rhythms was inferior:
more like the South—and childhood, for that
matter—as depicted by Hollywood or the
Broadway stage than the real thing itself. The
language of course is one of the real delights
of Mrs. Calhoun's book—its accuracy and fi-
delity of idiom and pattern but also its dramatic realization and revelation of the as-
sumptions of the whole world from which it

springs. Despite the occasional distractions of phonetic spellings, complete with bristling apostrophes reminiscent of Joel Chandler Harris, the language, no more than the work itself, is an export commodity, designed to vend the regional and the local to the big buying public of the outside world. Here it goes beyond the merely imitative or decorative and becomes a functional part of the living world of the novel itself. It's not for export, and it's not for sale. In Mrs. Calhoun's case, the language *is* part of the novel. And it is a joy.

Joy. That is the word which comes most readily to mind when we think about *Miss Minerva and William Green Hill*. It is the joy of childhood, the joy of life itself—but seen as all the more joyful because, always, we are aware of the sadness and sorrow which may lurk offstage and which sooner or later must be dealt with. The final enemy here is perhaps not so much adult decorum as the killer time itself, and he will finally win; we make no mistake about that. Yet we can meet him with a light heart and with the spirits of those who have become—or remained—as little children, if we would have the last word. And it's this joy, this quality of the debonair which Mrs. Calhoun's work embodies and inculcates. It's a great gift Mrs. Calhoun has given us, and I like to think she must have experienced great joy in its composition. We must be sorry only that she did not live to know our own enjoyment of her very joyful work.

—Robert Drake

ACKNOWLEDGMENTS

A substantial portion of the introduction appeared originally in an essay, "Two Old Juveniles," in *The Georgia Review* for Winter, 1959. I wish to express my appreciation to the editors of that publication for allowing me to draw heavily on that essay here.

I wish to record my thanks also to Mrs. Peyton Smith, Mrs. D. L. Goddard, Mrs. Edwin H. Brown, and Mrs. Sam C. Shelton, all of Covington, Tennessee, and to the Tipton County Public Library, also of Covington, for providing helpful information about Mrs. Frances Boyd Calhoun and her book and also to the staff of the Richmond Public Library, Richmond, Virginia, for information about Mrs. Emma Speed Sampson. I am indebted also to Mr. Henry Regnery of the Henry Regnery Company, Chicago, for answering a number of queries and also for his cordial interest in this project. Especial appreciation is extended to Mrs. Calhoun's nephew, Mr. Townes Boyd Johnson of Gallatin, Tennessee, who, on behalf of the heirs of Frances Boyd Calhoun, gave permission to reprint this work.

This facsimile of *Miss Minerva and Wil-*

liam Green Hill is reproduced from an edition in the University of Tennessee Library, Knoxville.

—R.D.

MISS MINERVA
AND WILLIAM GREEN HILL

MISS MINERVA and
WILLIAM GREEN HILL

CHAPTER I

A SCANDALIZED VIRGIN

THE bus drove up to the gate and stopped under the electric street-light. Perched on the box by the big, black negro driver sat a little boy whose slender figure was swathed in a huge rain coat.

Miss Minerva was on the porch waiting to receive him.

"Mercy on me, child," she said, "what on earth made you ride up there? Why did n't you get inside?"

"I jest wanted to ride by Sam Lamb," replied the child as he was lifted down. "An' I see a nice fat little man name' Major ——"

"He jes' would n' ride inside, Miss Minerva," interrupted the driver, quickly, to pass over the blush that rose to the spinster's thin cheek at mention of the Major.

"T wan't no use fer ter try ter make him ride
nowhars but jes' up by me. He jes' 'fused
an' 'fused an' 'sputed an' 'sputed; he jes'
tuck ter me f'om de minute he got off 'm de
train an' sot eyes on me; he am one easy chile
ter git 'quainted wid; so, I jes' h'isted him
up by me. Here am his verlise, ma'am."

"Good-bye, Sam Lamb," said the child as
the negro got back on the box and gathered
up the reins. "I 'll see you to-morrer."

Miss Minerva imprinted a thin, old-maid
kiss on the sweet, childish mouth. "I am
your Aunt Minerva," she said, as she picked
up his satchel.

The little boy carelessly drew the back of
his hand across his mouth.

"What are you doing?" she asked. "Are
you wiping my kiss off?"

"Naw 'm," he replied, "I 's jest a — I 's
a-rubbin' it in, I reckon."

"Come in, William," and his aunt led the
way through the wide hall into a big bed-
room.

"Billy, ma'am," corrected her nephew.

"William," firmly repeated Miss Minerva.
"You may have been called Billy on that
plantation where you were allowed to run
wild with the negroes, but your name is

William Green Hill and I shall insist upon your being called by it."

She stooped to help him off with his coat, remarking as she did so, "What a big overcoat; it is several sizes too large for you."

"Darned if 't ain't," agreed the child promptly.

"Who taught you such a naughty word?" she asked in a horrified voice. "Don't you know it is wrong to curse?"

"You call that cussin'?" came in scornful tones from the little boy. "You don't know cussin' when you see it; you jest oughter hear ole Uncle Jimmy-Jawed Jup'ter, Aunt Cindy's husban'; he 'll show you somer the pretties' cussin' you ever did hear."

"Who is Aunt Cindy?"

"She 's the colored 'oman what 'tends to me ever sence me an' Wilkes Booth Lincoln 's born, an' Uncle Jup'ter is her husban' an' he sho' is a stingeree on cussin'. Is yo' husban' much of a cusser?" he inquired.

A pale pink dyed Miss Minerva's thin, sallow face.

"I am not a married woman," she replied, curtly, "and I most assuredly would not permit any oaths to be used on my premises."

"Well, Uncle Jimmy-Jawed Jup'ter is jest

nach'elly boun' to cuss,— he's got a reperta-
tion to keep up," said Billy.

He sat down in a chair in front of his
aunt, crossed his legs and smiled confiden-
tially up into her face.

"Hell an' damn is jest easy ev'y day words
to that nigger. I wish you could hear him
cuss on a Sunday jest one time, Aunt Minerva; he'd sho' make you open yo' eyes an'
take in yo' sign. But Aunt Cindy don't 'low
me an' Wilkes Booth Lincoln to say nothin'
't all only jest 'darn' tell we gits grown
mens, an' puts on long pants."

"Wilkes Booth Lincoln?" questioned his
aunt.

"Ain't you never hear teller him?" asked
the child. "He's ole Aunt Blue-Gum
Tempy's Peruny Pearline's boy; an' Peruny
Pearline," he continued enthusiastically,
"she ain't no ord'nary nigger, her hair ain't
got nare kink an' she's got the grandes'
clo'es. They ain't nothin' snide 'bout her.
She got ten chillens an' ev'y single one of
'em's got a diff'unt pappy, she been married
so much. They do say she got Injun blood
in her, too."

Miss Minerva, who had been standing
prim, erect, and stiff, fell limply into a con-

venient rocking chair, and looked closely at this orphaned nephew who had come to live with her.

She saw a beautiful, bright, attractive, little face out of which big, saucy, grey eyes shaded by long curling black lashes looked

winningly at her; she saw a sweet, childish, red mouth, a mass of short, yellow curls, and a thin but graceful little figure.

"I knows the names of aller ole Aunt Blue-Gum Tempy's Peruny Pearline's chillens," he was saying proudly: "Admiral Farragut Moses the Prophet Esquire, he's **the** bigges'; an' Alice Ann Maria Dan Step-

an'-Go-Fetch-It, she had to nuss all the res';
she say fas' as she git th'oo nussin' one an'
'low she goin' to have a breathin' spell here
come another one an' she got to nuss it.
An' the nex' is Mount Sinai Tabernicle, he
name fer the church where ol' Aunt Blue-
Gum Tempy's Peruny Pearline takes her
sackerment; an' the nex' is First Thessalonians; Second Thessalonians, he 's dead
an' gone to the Bad Place 'cause he skunt a
cat,— I don't mean skin the cat on a actin'
pole like me an' Wilkes Booth Lincoln does,
— he skunt a sho' 'nough cat what was a
black cat, what was a ole witch, an' she come
back an' ha'nt him an' he growed thinner
an' thinner an' weasler an' weasler, tell finely
he wan't nothin' 't all but a skel'ton, an' the
Bad Man won't 'low nobody 't all to give
his parch' tongue no water, an' he got to,
ever after amen, be toast on a pitchfork.
An' Oleander Magnolia Althea is the nex',"
he continued, enumerating Peruny Pearline's offspring on his thin, well molded
fingers, "she got the seven-year itch; an'
Gettysburg, an' Biddle-&-Brothers-Mercan-
tile-Co.; he name fer the sto' where ole Aunt
Blue-Gum Tempy's Peruny Pearline gits
credit so she can pay when she fetches in

her cotton in the fall; an' Wilkes Booth Lincoln, him an' me 's twins, we was borned
the same day only I 's borned to my mama
an' he's borned to his 'n an' Doctor Jen-
kins fetched me an' Doctor Shacklefoot
fetched him. An' Decimus Ultimus,"— the
little boy triumphantly put his right forefinger on his left little one, thus making the
tenth, "she 's the baby an' she 's got the
colic an' cries loud 'nough to wake up Israel;
Wilkes Booth Lincoln say he wish the little
devil would die. Peruny Pearline firs' name
her 'Doctor Shacklefoot' 'cause he fetches
all her chillens, but the doctor he say that
ain't no name fer a girl, so he name her
Decimus Ultimus."

Miss Minerva, sober, proper, dignified, religious old maid unused to children, listened
in frozen amazement and paralyzed silence.
She decided to put the child to bed at once
that she might collect her thoughts, and lay
some plans for the rearing of this sadly neglected, little orphaned nephew.

"William," she said, "it is bedtime, and
I know you must be sleepy after your long
ride on the cars. Would you like something
to eat before I put you to bed? I saved you
some supper."

"Naw 'm, I ain't hongry; the Major man what I talk to on the train tuck me in the dinin'-room an' gimme all I could hol'; I jest eat an' eat tell they wan't a wrinkle in me," was the reply. "He axed me 'bout you, too. Is he name' Major Minerva?"

She opened a door in considerable confusion, and they entered a small, neat room adjoining.

"This is your own little room, William," said she, "you see it opens into mine. Have you a night-shirt?"

"Naw 'm, I don' need no night-shirt. I jest sleeps in my unions and sometimes in my overalls."

"Well, you may sleep in your union suit to-night," said his scandalized relative, "and I 'll see what I can do for you to-morrow. Can you undress yourself?"

Her small nephew wrinkled his nose, disdainfully. "Well, I reckon so," he scornfully made answer. "Me an' Wilkes Booth Lincoln been undressin' usself ever sence we 's born."

"I 'll come in here after a while and turn off the light. Good-night, William."

"Good-night, Aunt Minerva," responded the little boy.

CHAPTER II

THE RABBIT'S LEFT HIND FOOT

A FEW minutes later, as Miss Minerva sat rocking and thinking, the door opened and a lean, graceful, little figure, clad in a skinny, grey union suit, came into the room.

"Ain't I a-goin' to say no prayers?" demanded a sweet, childish voice. "Aunt Cindy hear me an' Wilkes Booth Lincoln say us prayers ev'y night sence we 's born."

"Why, of course you must say your prayers," said his aunt, blushing at having to be reminded of her duty by this young heathen; "kneel down here by me."

Billy looked at his aunt's bony frame and thought of Aunt Cindy's soft, fat, ample lap. A wistful look crossed his childish face as he dropped down in front of her and laid his head against her knee, then the bright, beautiful little face took on an angelic ex-

pression as he closed his eyes and softly
chanted:

"'Now I lays me down to sleep,
I prays the Lord my soul to keep,
If I should die befo' I wake,
I prays the Lord my soul to take.

"'Keep way f'om me hoodoo an' witch,
Lead my paf f'om the po'-house gate,
I pines fer the golden harps an' sich,
Oh, Lord, I 'll set an' pray an' wait.'
"Oh, Lord, bless ev'ybody; bless me an'
Aunt Cindy, an' Wilkes Booth Lincoln, an'

Aunt Blue-Gum Tempy's Peruny Pearline, an' Uncle Jimmy-Jawed Jup'ter, an' ev'ybody, an' Sam Lamb, an' Aunt Minerva, an' aller Aunt Blue-Gum Tempy's Peruny Pearline's chillens, an' give Aunt Minerva a billy goat or a little nanny if she 'd ruther, an' bless Major Minerva, an' make me a good boy like Sanctified Sophy, fer Jesus' sake. Amen."

"What is that you have tied around your neck, William?" she asked, as the little boy rose to his feet.

"That 's my rabbit foot; you won't never have no 'sease 't all an' nobody can't never conjure you if you wears a rabbit foot. This here one is the lef' hin' foot; it was ketched by a red-headed nigger with cross-eyes in a graveyard at twelve er'clock on a Friday night, when they 's a full moon. He give it to Aunt Cindy to tie 'roun' my nake when I 's a baby. Ain't you got no rabbit foot?" he anxiously inquired.

"No," she answered. "I have never had one and I have never been conjured either. Give it to me, William; I can not allow you to be so superstitious," and she held out her hand.

"Please, Aunt Minerva, jest lemme wear

it to-night," he pleaded. "Me an' Wilkes Booth Lincoln 's been wearin' us rabbit foots ever sence we 's born."

"No," she said firmly; "I 'll put a stop to such nonsense at once. Give it to me, William."

Billy looked at his aunt's austere countenance and lovingly fingered his charm; he opened his mouth to say something, but hesitated; slowly he untied the string around his neck and laid his treasure on her lap; then without looking up, he ran into his own little room, closing the door behind him.

Soon afterward Miss Minerva, hearing a sound like a stifled sob coming from the adjoining room, opened the door softly and looked into a sad, little face with big, wide, open eyes shining with tears.

"What is the matter, William?" she coldly asked.

"I ain't never slep' by myself," he sobbed. "Wilkes Booth Lincoln always sleep on a pallet by my bed ever sence we 's born an'— an' I wants Aunt Cindy to tell me 'bout Uncle Piljerk Peter."

His aunt sat down on the bed by his side. She was not versed in the ways of childhood

and could not know that the little boy
wanted to pillow his head on Aunt Cindy's
soft and ample bosom, that he was home-
sick for his black friends, the only companions he had ever known.

"I 'll tell you a Bible story," she tempor-
ized. "You must not be a baby. You are
not afraid, are you, William? God is always
with you."

"I don' want no God," he sullenly made
reply, "I wants somebody with sho' 'nough
skin an' bones, an'— an' I wants to hear
'bout Uncle Piljerk Peter."

"I will tell you a Bible story," again suggested his aunt, "I will tell you about ——"

"I don' want to hear no Bible story,
neither," he objected, "I wants to hear Uncle
Jimmy-Jawed Jup'ter play his 'corjun an'
sing:

" 'Rabbit up the gum tree, Coon is in the
      holler

Wake, snake; Juney-Bug stole a half a
      dollar.' "

"I 'll sing you a hymn," said Miss Minerva
patiently.

"I don' want to hear you sing no hymn,"
said Billy impolitely. "I wants to see Sanctified Sophy shout."

As his aunt could think of no substitute
with which to tempt him in lieu of Sanctified
Sophy's shouting, she remained silent.

"An' I wants Wilkes Booth Lincoln to
dance a clog," persisted her nephew.

Miss Minerva still remained silent. She
felt unable to cope with the situation till she
had adjusted her thoughts and made her
plans.

Presently Billy, looking at her shrewdly,
said:

"Gimme my rabbit foot, Aunt Minerva,
an' I 'll go right off to sleep."

When she again looked in on him he was
fast asleep, a rosy flush on his babyish, tear-
stained cheek, his red lips half parted, his
curly head pillowed on his arm, and close
against his soft, young throat there nestled
the left hind foot of a rabbit.

Miss Minerva's bed time was half after
nine o'clock, summer or winter. She had
hardly varied a second in the years that had
elapsed since the runaway marriage of her
only relative, the young sister whose child
had now come to live with her. But on the
night of Billy's arrival the stern, narrow
woman sat for hours in her rocking chair,

her mind busy with thoughts of that pretty young sister, dead since the boy's birth.

And now the wild, reckless, dissipated brother-in-law was dead, too, and the child had been sent to her; to the aunt who did not want him, who did not care for children, who had never forgiven her sister her unfortunate marriage. "If he had only been a girl," she sighed. What she believed to be a happy thought entered her brain.

"I shall rear him," she promised herself, "just as if he were a little girl; then he will be both a pleasure and a comfort to me, and a companion for my loneliness."

Miss Minerva was strictly methodical; she worked ever by the clock, so many hours for this, so many minutes for that. William, she now resolved, for the first time becoming really interested in him, should grow up to be a model young man, a splendid and wonderful piece of mechanism, a fine, practical, machine-like individual, moral, upright, religious. She was glad that he was young; she would begin his training on the morrow. She would teach him to sew, to sweep, to churn, to cook, and when he was older he should be educated for the ministry.

"Yes," said Miss Minerva; "I shall be very

strict with him just at first, and punish him
for the slightest disobedience or misde-
meanor, and he will soon learn that my au-
thority is not to be questioned."

And the little boy who had never had a
restraining hand laid upon him in his short
life? He slept sweetly and innocently in
the next room dreaming of the care-free ex-
istence on the plantation and of his idle,
happy, negro companions.

CHAPTER III

THE WILLING WORKER

ET up, William," said Miss Minerva, "and come with me to the bath-room; I have fixed your bath."

The child's sleepy eyes popped wide open at this astounding command.

"Ain't this-here Wednesday?" he asked sharply.

"Yes; to-day is Wednesday. Hurry up or your water will get cold."

"Well, me an' Wilkes Booth Lincoln jest washed las' Sat'day. We ain't got to wash no mo' till nex' Sat'day," he argued.

"Oh, yes," said his relative; "you must bathe every day."

"Me an' Wilkes Booth Lincoln ain't never wash on a Wednesday sence we 's born," he protested indignantly.

Billy's idea of a bath was taken from the severe weekly scrubbing which Aunt Cindy gave him with a hard washrag, and he felt that he 'd rather die at once than have to bathe every day.

He followed his aunt dolefully to the bath-room at the end of the long back-porch of the old-fashioned, one-story house; but once in the big white tub he was delighted.

In fact he stayed in it so long Miss Minerva had to knock on the door and tell him to hurry up and get ready for breakfast.

"Say," he yelled out to her, "I likes this-here; it 's mos' as fine as Johnny's Wash Hole where me and' Wilkes Booth Lincoln goes in swimmin' ever sence we 's born."

When he came into the dining-room he was a sight to gladden even a prim old maid's heart. The water had curled his hair into riotous yellow ringlets, his bright eyes gleamed, his beautiful, expressive little face shone happily, and every movement of his agile, lithe figure was grace itself.

"I sho' is hongry," he remarked, as he took his seat at the breakfast table.

Miss Minerva realized that now was the time to begin her small nephew's training; if she was ever to teach him to speak correctly she must begin at once.

"William," she said sternly, "you must

not talk so much like a negro. Instead of saying 'I sho' is hongry,' you should say, 'I am very hungry.' Listen to me and try to speak more correctly."

"Don't! don't!" she screamed as he helped himself to the meat and gravy, leaving a little brown river on her fresh white table-cloth. "Wait until I ask a blessing; then I will help you to what you want."

Billy enjoyed his breakfast very much. "These muffins sho' is —" he began; catching his aunt's eye he corrected himself: "These muffins am very good."

"These muffins are very good," said Miss Minerva patiently.

"Did you ever eat any bobbycued rabbit?" he asked. "Me an' Wilkes Booth Lincoln been eatin' chit'lin's, an' sweet 'taters, an' 'possum, an' squirrel, an' hoe-cake, an' Brunswick stew ever sence we 's born," was his proud announcement.

"Use your napkin," commanded she, "and don't fill your mouth so full."

The little boy flooded his plate with syrup.

"These-here 'lasses sho' is —" he began, but instantly remembering that he must be more particular in his speech, he stammered out:

"These-here sho' is — am — are a nice messer 'lasses. I ain't never eat sech a good bait. They sho' is — I aimed to say — these 'lasses sho' are a bird; they 's 'nother sight tastier 'n sorghum, an' Aunt Cindy 'lows that sorghum is the very penurity of a nigger."

She did not again correct him.

"I must be very patient," she thought, "and go very slowly. I must not expect too much of him at first."

After breakfast Miss Minerva, who would not keep a servant, preferring to do her own work, tied a big cook-apron around the little boy's neck, and told him to churn while she washed the dishes. This arrangement did not suit Billy.

"Boys don't churn," he said sullenly, "me an' Wilkes Booth Lincoln don' never have to churn sence we 's born; 'omans has to churn an' I ain't a-going to. Major Minerva — he ain't never churn," he began belligerently but his relative turned an uncompromising and rather perturbed back upon him. Realizing that he was beaten, he submitted to his fate, clutched the dasher angrily, and began his weary work.

He was glad his little black friend did not witness his disgrace.

As he thought of Wilkes Booth Lincoln the big tears came into his eyes and rolled down his cheeks; he leaned way over the churn and the great glistening tears splashed right into the hole made for the dasher, and rolled into the milk.

Billy grew interested at once and laughed aloud; he puckered up his face and tried to weep again, for he wanted more tears to fall into the churn; but the tears refused to come and he could n't squeeze another one out of his eyes.

"Aunt Minerva," he said mischievously, "I done ruint yo' buttermilk."

"What have you done?" she inquired.

"It 's done ruint," he replied, "you 'll hafter th'ow it away; 't ain't fitten fer nothin.' I done cried 'bout a bucketful in it."

"Why did you cry?" asked Miss Minerva calmly. "Don't you like to work?"

"Yes 'm, I jes' loves to work; I wish I had time to work all the time. But it makes my belly ache to churn,— I got a awful pain right now."

"Churn on!" she commanded unsympathetically.

He grabbed the dasher and churned vigorously for one minute.

"I reckon the butter 's done come," he
announced, resting from his labors.

"It has n't begun to come yet," replied the
exasperated woman. "Don't waste so much
time, William."

The child churned in silence for the space
of two minutes, and suggested: "It 's time to
put hot water in it; Aunt Cindy always puts
hot water in it. Lemme git some fer you."

"I never put hot water in my milk," said
she, "it makes the butter puffy. Work more
and talk less, William."

Again there was a brief silence, broken
only by the sound of the dasher thumping
against the bottom of the churn, and the
rattle of the dishes.

"I sho' is tired," he presently remarked,
heaving a deep sigh. "My arms is 'bout give
out, Aunt Minerva. Ole Aunt Blue-Gum
Tempy's Peruny Pearline see a man churn
with his toes; lemme git a chair an' see if
I can't churn with my toes."

"Indeed you shall not," responded his an-
noyed relative positively.

"Sanctified Sophy knowed a colored 'oman
what had a little dog went roun' an' roun'

an' churn fer her," remarked Billy after a short pause. "If you had a billy goat or a little nanny I could hitch him to the churn fer you ev'ry day."

"William," commanded his aunt, "don't

say another word until you have finished your work."

"Can't I sing?" he asked.

She nodded permission as she went through the open door into the dining-room.

Returning a few minutes later she found

him sitting astride the churn, using the dasher so vigorously that buttermilk was splashing in every direction, and singing in a clear, sweet voice:

"He'll feed you when you's naked,
   The orphan stear he'll dry,
   He'll clothe you when you's hongry
   An' take you when you die."

Miss Minerva jerked him off with no gentle hand.

"What I done now?" asked the boy innocently. "'T ain't no harm as I can see jes' to straddle a churn."

"Go out in the front yard," commanded his aunt, "and sit in the swing till I call you. I'll finish the work without your assistance. And, William," she called after him, "there is a very bad little boy who lives next door; I want you to have as little to do with him as possible."

CHAPTER IV

SWEETHEART AND PARTNER

BILLY was sitting quietly in the big lawn-swing when his aunt, dressed for the street, finally came through the front door.

"I am going up-town, William," she said, "I want to buy you some things that you may go with me to church Sunday. Have you ever been to Sunday-School?"

"Naw 'm; but I been to pertracted meetin'," came the ready response, "I see Sanctified Sophy shout tell she tore ev'y rag offer her back 'ceptin' a shimmy. She's one 'oman what sho' is got 'ligion; she ain't never backslid 't all, an' she ain't never fell f'om grace but one time ——"

"Stay right in the yard till I come back. Sit in the swing and don't go outside the front yard. I shan't be gone long," said Miss Minerva.

His aunt had hardly left the gate before Billy caught sight of a round, fat little face peering at him through the palings which separated Miss Minerva's yard from that of her next-door neighbor.

"Hello!" shouted Billy. "Is you the bad little boy what can't play with me?"

"What you doing in Miss Minerva's yard?" came the answering interrogation across the fence.

"I 's come to live with her," replied Billy. "My mama an' papa is dead. What 's yo' name?"

"I 'm Jimmy Garner. How old are you? I 'm most six, I am."

"Shucks, I 's already six, a-going on seven. Come on, le's swing."

"Can't," said the new acquaintance, "I 've runned off once to-day, and got licked for it."

"I ain't never got no whippin' sence me an' Wilkes Booth Lincoln 's born," boasted Billy.

"Ain't you?" asked Jimmy. "I 'spec' I been whipped more 'n a million times, my mama is so pertic'lar with me. She 's 'bout the pertic'larest woman ever was; she don't 'low me to leave the yard 'thout I get a whipping. I believe I will come over to see you 'bout half a minute."

Suiting the action to the word Jimmy climbed the fence, and the two little boys were soon comfortably settled facing each other in the big lawn-swing.

"Who lives over there?" asked Billy, pointing to the house across the street.

"That's Miss Cecilia's house. That's her coming out of the front gate now."

The young lady smiled and waved her hand at them.

"Ain't she a peach?" asked Jimmy. "She's my sweetheart and she is 'bout the swellest sweetheart they is."

"She's mine, too," promptly replied Billy, who had fallen in love at first sight. "I's a-goin' to have her fer my sweetheart too."

"Naw, she ain't yours, neither; she's mine," angrily declared the other little boy, kicking his rival's legs. "You all time talking 'bout you going to have Miss Cecilia for your sweetheart. She's done already promised me."

"I'll tell you what," proposed Billy, "lemme have her an' you can have Aunt Minerva."

"I wouldn't have Miss Minerva to save

your life," replied Jimmy disrespectfully,
"her nake ain't no bigger 'n that," making a
circle of his thumb and forefinger. "Miss
Cecilia, Miss Cecilia," he shrieked tantaliz-
ingly, "is my sweetheart."

"I 'll betcher I have her fer a sweetheart
soon as ever I see her," said Billy.

"What 's your name?" asked Jimmy presently.

"Aunt Minerva says it 's William Green
Hill, but 't ain't, it 's jest plain Billy," responded the little boy.

"Ain't God a nice, good old man," remarked Billy, after they had swung in
silence for a while, with an evident desire to
make talk.

"That He is," replied Jimmy, enthusiastically. "He 's 'bout the forgivingest person
ever was. I just could n't get 'long at all
'thout Him. It don't make no differ'nce
what you do or how many times you run off,
all you got to do is just ask God to forgive
you and tell him you 're sorry and ain't
going to do so no more, that night when you
say your prayers, and it 's all right with God.
S'posing He was one of these wants-his-
own-way kind o' mans, He could make
Hi'self the troublesomest person ever was,

and little boys could n't do nothing a tall. I sure think a heap of God. He ain't never give me the worst of it yet."

"I wonder what He looks like," mused Billy.

"I s'pec' He just looks like the three-head-ed giant in Jack the Giant-Killer," explained Jimmy, "'cause He 's got three heads and one body. His heads are name' Papa, Son, and Holy Ghost, and His body is just name' plain God. Miss Cecilia 'splained it all to me and she is 'bout the splendidest 'splainer they is. She 's my Sunday-School teacher."

"She 's goin' to be my Sunday-School teacher, too," said Billy serenely.

"Yours nothing; you all time want my Sunday-School teacher."

"Jimmee!" called a voice from the interior of the house in the next yard.

"Somebody 's a-callin' you," said Billy.

"That ain't nobody but mama," explained Jimmy composedly.

"Jimmee-ee!" called the voice.

"Don't make no noise," warned that little boy, "maybe she 'll give up toreckly."

"You Jimmee!" his mother called again.

Jimmy made no move to leave the swing.

"I don' never have to go 'less she says

'James Lafayette Garner,' then I got to hustle," he remarked.

"Jimmy Garner!"

"She 's mighty near got me," he said softly; "but maybe she 'll get tired and won't call no more. She ain't plumb mad yet."

"James Garner!"

"It 's coming now," said Jimmy dolefully.

The two little boys sat very still and quiet.

"James Lafayette Garner!"

The younger child sprang to his feet.

"I got to get a move on now," he said; "when she calls like that she means business. I betcher she 's got a switch and a hair-brush and a slipper in her hand right this minute. I 'll be back toreckly," he promised.

He was as good as his word, and in a very short time he was sitting again facing Billy in the swing.

"She just wanted to know where her embroid'ry scissors was," he explained. "It don't matter what 's lost in that house I 'm always the one that 's got to be 'sponsible and all time got to go look for it."

"Did you find 'em?" asked Billy.

"Yep; I went right straight where I left

'em yeste'day. I had 'em trying to cut a piece of wire. I stole off and went down to Sam Lamb's house this morning and tooken breakfast with him and his old woman, Sukey," he boasted.

"I knows Sam Lamb," said Billy, "I rode up on the bus with him."

"He's my partner," remarked Jimmy.

"He's mine, too," said Billy quickly.

"No, he ain't neither; you all time talking 'bout you going to have Sam Lamb for a partner. You want everything I got. You want Miss Cecilia and you want Sam Lamb. Well, you just ain't a-going to have 'em. You got to get somebody else for your partner and sweetheart."

"Well, you jest wait an' see," said Billy. "I got Major Minerva."

"Shucks, they ain't no Major name' that away," and Jimmy changed the subject. "Sam Lamb's sow's got seven little pigs. He lemme see 'em suck," said Sam Lamb's partner proudly. "He's got a cow, too; she's got the worrisomest horns ever was. I believe she's a steer anyway."

"Shucks," said the country boy, contemptuously, "You do' know a steer when you see one; you can't milk no steer."

CHAPTER V

TURNING ON THE HOSE

"LOOK! Ain't that a snake?" shrieked Billy, pointing to what looked to him like a big snake coiled in the yard.

"Snake, nothing!" sneered his companion, "that 's a hose. You all time got to call a hose a snake. Come on, let 's sprinkle," and Jimmy sprang out of the swing, jerked up the hose, and dragged it to the hydrant. "My mama don't never 'low me to sprinkle with her hose, but Miss Minerva she 's so good I don' reckon she 'll care," he cried mendaciously.

Billy followed, watched his companion screw the hose to the faucet, and turn the water on. There was a hissing, gurgling sound and a stream of water shot out, much to the rapture of the astonished Billy.

"Won't Aunt Minerva care?" he asked, anxiously. "Is she a real 'ligious 'oman?"

"She is the Christianest woman they is,"

announced the other child. "Come on, we'll
sprinkle the street—and I don't want nobody
to get in our way neither."

"I wish Wilkes Booth Lincoln could see
us," said Miss Minerva's nephew.

A big, fat negress, with a bundle of clothes
tied in a red table cloth on her head, came
waddling down the sidewalk.

Billy looked at Jimmy and giggled: Jimmy

looked at Billy and giggled; then, the latter
took careful aim and a stream of water hit
the old woman squarely in the face.

"Who dat? What's yo' doin'?" she yelled,
as she backed off. 'I's a-gwine to tell yo'

pappy, Jimmy Garner," as she recognized one of the culprits. "P'int dat ar ho'e 'way f'om me, 'fo' I make yo' ma spank yuh slab-sided. I got to git home an' wash. Drap it, I tell yuh!"

Two little girls rolling two doll buggies in which reposed two enormous rag-babies were seen approaching.

"That 's Lina Hamilton and Frances Black," said Jimmy, "they 're my chums."

Billy took a good look at them. "They 's goin' to be my chums, too," he said calmly.

"Your chums, nothing!" angrily cried Jimmy, swelling up pompously. "You all time trying to claim my chums. I can't have nothing a tall 'thout you got to stick your mouth in. You 'bout the selfishest boy they is. You want everything I got, all time."

The little girls were now quite near and Jimmy hailed them gleefully, forgetful of his anger:

"Come on, Lina, you and Frances," he shrieked, "and we can have the mostest fun. Billy here 's done come to live with Miss Minerva and she 's done gone up town and don't care if we sprinkle, 'cause she 's got so much 'ligion."

"But you know none of us are allowed to use a hose," objected Lina.

"But it 's so much fun," said Jimmy; "and Miss Minerva she 's so Christian she ain't going to raise much of a rough-house, and if she do we can run when we see her coming."

"I can't run," said Billy, "I ain't got nowhere to run to an'——"

"If that ain't just like you, Billy," interrupted Jimmy, "all time talking 'bout you ain't got nowhere to run to; you don't want nobody to have no fun. You 'bout the picayunest boy they is."

Little Ikey Rosenstein, better known as "Goose-Grease," dressed in a cast-off suit of his big brother's, with his father's hat set rakishly back on his head and over his ears, was coming proudly down the street some distance off.

"Yonder comes Goose-Grease Rosenstein," said Jimmy gleefully. "When he gets right close le's make him hop."

"All right," agreed Billy, his good humor restored, "le's baptize him good."

"Oh, we can't baptize him," exclaimed the other little boy, " 'cause he 's a Jew and the Bible says not to baptize Jews. You got to mesmerize 'em. How come me to know

so much?" he continued condescendingly,
"Miss Cecilia teached me in the Sunday-
School. Sometimes I know so much I
I feel like I'm going to bust. She teached
me 'bout 'Scuffle little chillens and forbid
'em not,' and 'bout 'Ananias telled Sapphira
he done it with his little hatchet,' and 'bout
''Lijah jumped over the moon in a auto-
mobile.' I know everything what's in the
Bible. Miss Cecilia sure is a cracker-jack;
she's 'bout the stylishest Sunday-School
teacher they is."

"'T was the cow jumped over the moon,"
said Frances, "and it is n't in the Bible; it's
in Mother Goose."

"And Elijah went to Heaven in a chariot
of fire," corrected Lina.

"And I know all 'bout Gabr'el," continued
Jimmy unabashed. "When folks called him
to blow his trumpet he was under the hay-
stack fast asleep."

Ikey was quite near by this time to command the attention of the four children.

"Let's mesmerize Goose-Grease," yelled
Jimmy, as he turned the stream of water full
upon him.

Frances, Lina, and Billy clapped their
hands and laughed for joy.

With a terrified and angry shriek their victim, dripping water at every step, ran howling by his tormentors. When he reached a safe distance he turned around, shook a fist at them, and screamed back:

"My papa is going to have you all arrested and locked up in the calaboose."

"Calaboose, nothing!" jeered Jimmy. "You all time wanting to put somebody in the calaboose 'cause they mesmerize you. You got to be mesmerized 'cause it's in the Bible."

A short, stout man, dressed in neat black clothes, was coming toward them.

"Oh, that's the Major!" screamed Billy delightedly, taking the hose and squaring himself to greet his friend of the train, but Jimmy jerked it out of his hand, before either of them noticed him turning about, as if for something forgotten.

"You ain't got the sense of a one-eyed tadpole, Billy," he said. "That's Miss Minerva's beau. He's been loving her more 'n a million years. My mama says he ain't never going to marry nobody a tall 'thout he can get Miss Minerva, and Miss Minerva she just turns up her nose at anything that wears pants. You better not sprinkle him.

He's been to the war and got his big toe shot off. He kilt 'bout a million Injuns and Yankees and he's name' Major 'cause he's a Confed'rit vetrun. He went to the war when he ain't but fourteen."

"Did he have on long pants?" asked Billy. "I call him Major Minerva —"

"Gladys Maude's got the pennyskeeters," broke in Frances importantly, fussing over her baby, "and I'm going to see Doctor Sanford. Don't you think she looks pale, Jimmy?"

"Pale, nothing!" sneered the little boy. "Girls got to all time play their dolls are sick. Naw; I don't know nothing a tall 'bout your Gladys Maude."

Lina gazed up the street.

"That looks like Miss Minerva to me 'way up yonder," she remarked. "I think we had better get away from here before she sees us."

Two little girls rolling two doll buggies fairly flew down the street and one little boy quickly climbed to the top of the dividing fence. From this safe vantage point he shouted to Billy, who was holding the nozzle of the hose out of which poured a stream of water.

"You 'd better turn that water off 'cause Miss Minerva 's going to be madder 'n a green persimmon."

"I do' know how to," said Billy forlornly. "You turnt it on."

"Drop the hose and run to the hydrant and twist that little thing at the top," screamed Jimmy. "You all time got to per-pose someping to get little boys in trouble anyway," he added ungenerously.

"You perposed this yo'self," declared an indignant Billy. "You said Aunt Minerva 's so 'ligious she would n't git mad."

"Christian womans can get just as mad as any other kind," declared the other boy, sliding from his perch on the fence and run-ning across his lawn to disappear behind his own front door.

Holding her skirts nearly up to her knees Miss Minerva stepped gingerly along the wet and muddy street till she got to her gate, where her nephew met her, looking a little guilty, but still holding his head up with that characteristic, manly air which was so at-tractive.

"William," she said sternly, "I see you have been getting into mischief, and I feel it my duty to punish you, so that you may

learn to be trustworthy. I said nothing to
you about the hose because I did not think
you would know how to use it."

Billy remained silent. He did not want to
betray his little companions of the morning,
so he said nothing in his own defense.

"Come with me into the house," continued
his aunt, "you must go to bed at once."

But the child protested vigorously.

"Don' make me go to bed in the daytime, Aunt Minerva; me an' Wilkes Booth
Lincoln ain't never went to bed in the daytime since we's born, an' I ain't never hear
tell of a real 'ligious 'oman a-puttin' a little
boy in bed 'fore it's dark; an' I ain't never
a-goin' to meddle with yo' ole hose no mo'."

But Miss Minerva was obdurate, and the
little boy spent a miserable hour between the
sheets.

CHAPTER VI

SUCCESSFUL STRATEGY.

I HAVE a present for you," said his aunt, handing Billy a long, rectangular package.

"Thank you, ma'am," said her beaming nephew as he sat down on the floor, all eager anticipation, and began to untie the string. His charming, changeful face was bright and happy again, but his expression became one of indignant amaze as he saw the contents of the box.

"What I want with a doll?" he asked angrily, "I ain't no girl."

"I think every little boy should have a doll and learn to make clothes for it," said Miss Minerva. "I don't want you to be a great, rough boy; I want you to be sweet and gentle like a little girl; I am going to teach you how to sew and cook and sweep, so you may grow up a comfort to me."

This was a gloomy forecast for the little

boy accustomed, as he had been, to the freedom of a big plantation, and he scowled
darkly.

"Me an' Wilkes Booth Lincoln ain't never
hafter play with no dolls sence we 's born,"
he replied sullenly, "we goes in swimmin' an'
plays baseball. I can knock a home-run an'
pitch a curve an' ketch a fly. Why don't
you gimme a baseball bat? I already got a
ball what Admiral Farragut gimme. An' I
ain't a-goin' to be no sissy neither. Lina
an' Frances plays dolls, me an' Jimmy ——"
he stopped in sudden confusion.

"Lina and Frances and James!" exclaimed
his aunt. "What do you know about them,
William?"

The child's face flushed. "I seen 'em this
mornin'," he acknowledged.

Miss Minerva put a hand on either shoulder and looked straight into his eyes.

"William, who started that sprinkling this
morning?" she questioned, sharply.

Billy flushed guiltily and lowered his eye-
lids; but only for an instant. Quickly re-
covering his composure he returned her gaze
steadily and ignored her question.

"I see yo' beau too, Aunt Minerva," he
remarked tranquilly.

It was Miss Minerva this time who lost her composure, for her thin, sallow face became perfectly crimson.

"My beau?" she asked confusedly. "Who put that nonsense into your head?"

"Jimmy show him to me," he replied jauntily, once more master of the situation and in full realization of the fact. "Why don't you marry him, Aunt Minerva, so 's he could live right here with us? An' I could learn him how to churn. I s'pec' he 'd make a beautiful churner. He sho' is a pretty little fat man," he continued flatteringly. "An' dress? That beau was jest dressed plumb up to the top notch. I sho' would marry him if I 's you an' not turn up my nose at him 'cause he wears pants, an' you can learn him how to talk properer 'n what he do an' I betcher he 'd jest nachelly take to a broom, an' I s'pec' he ain't got nobody 't all to show him how to sew. An' y' all could get the doctor to fetch you a little baby so he would n't hafter play with no doll. I sho' wisht we had him here," ended a selfish Billy, "he could save me a lot of steps. An' I sho' would like to hear 'bout all them Injuns an' Yankees what he 's killed."

Billy's aunt was visibly embarrassed.

The persistent admiration of this, her one lover, had been pleasing to her, yet she had never been willing to sacrifice her independence for the cares and trials of matrimony. The existing state of affairs between the two was known to every one in the small town, but such was Miss Minerva's dignified aloofness that Billy was the first person who had ever dared to broach the subject to her.

"Sit down here, William," she commanded, "and I will read to you."

"Tell me a tale," he said, looking up at her with his bright, sweet smile. The doll lay neglected on a chair near by and Billy wanted her to forget it.

"Tell me 'bout Piljerk Peter."

"Piljerk Peter?" there was an interrogation in her voice.

"Yas 'm. Ain't you never hear tell 'bout Piljerk Peter? He had fifteen chillens an' one time the las' one of 'em an' his ole 'oman was down with the fever an' he ain't got but one pill an' they so sick they mos' 'bout to die an' ain't nobody in the fiel' fer to pick the cotton an' he can't git no doctor an' he ain't got but jest that one pill; so he tie that pill to a string an' let the bigges' chile swaller it an' draw it back up an' let the nex'

chile swaller it an' jerk it back up an' let the
nex' chile swaller it an' jerk it back up an'
let the nex' chile swaller it an' jerk it back
up an' let the nex' ———."

"I don't believe in telling tales to children," interrupted his aunt, "I will tell you
biographical and historical stories and stories from the Bible.   Now listen, while I read
to you."

"An' the nex' chile swaller it an' he jerk
it back up," continued Billy serenely, "an'
the nex' chile swaller it an' he jerk it back
up tell finely ev'y single one of 'em, plumb
down to the baby, swaller that pill an' the
las' one of 'em got well an' that one pill it
done the work.   Then he tuck the pill and
give it to his ole 'oman an' she swaller it an'
he jerk it back up but did n't nothin' 't all
come up but jest the string an' his ole 'oman
she died 'cause all the strenk done gone
outer that pill."

Miss Minerva opened a book called "Gems
for the Household," which she had pur-
chased from a silver-tongued book-agent.
She selected an article the subject of which
was "The Pure in Heart."

Billy listened with a seemingly attentive
ear to the choice flow of words, but in reality

his little brain was busy with its own
thoughts. The article closed with the suggestion that if one were innocent and pure
he would have a dreamless sleep:

> "If you have a conscience clear,
>   And God's commands you keep;
> If your heart is good and pure,
>   You will have a perfect sleep."

Billy's aunt concluded. Wishing to know
if he had understood what she had just read
she asked:

"What people sleep the soundest?"

"Niggers," was his prompt reply, as he
thought of the long summer days and the
colored folk on the plantation.

She was disappointed, but not discouraged.

"Now, William," she admonished, "I 'm
going to read you another piece, and I want
you to tell me about it, when I get through.
Pay strict attention."

"Yas 'm," he readily agreed.

She chose an article describing the keen
sense of smell in animals. Miss Minerva
was not an entertaining reader and the words
were long and fairly incomprehensible to
the little boy sitting patiently at her side.

Again his thoughts wandered, though every now and then he caught a word or two.

"What animals have the keenest sense of smell, William?" was her query at the conclusion of her reading.

"Billy goats," was Billy's answer without the slightest hesitation.

"You have goats on the brain," she said in anger. "I did not read one word about billy goats."

"Well, if 't aint a billy goat," he replied, "I do' know what 't is 'thout it 's a skunk."

"I bought you a little primer this morning," she remarked after a short silence, "and I want you to say a lesson every day."

"I already knows a lot," he boasted. "Tabernicle, he an' Mercantile both been to school an' they learnt me an' Wilkes Booth Lincoln. I knows crooked S, an' broken back K, an' curly tail Q, an' roun' O, an' I can spell c-a-t cat, an' d-o-g dog an' A stands fer apple."

That night he concluded his ever lengthy prayer at his kinswoman's knee with:

"O Lord, please make for Aunt Minerva a little baby, make her two of 'em. O Lord,

if you got 'em to spare please make her
three little babies an' let 'em all be girls so 's
she can learn 'em how to churn an' sew.
An' bless Aunt Minerva and Major Minerva,
f'r ever 'nd ever. Amen."

As he rose from his knees he asked:
"Aunt Minerva, do God work on Sunday?"

"No-o," answered his relative, hesitat-
ingly.

"Well, it look like He 'd jest hafter work
on Sunday, He 's so busy jest a-makin'
babies. He makes all the niggers an'
heathens an' Injuns an' white chillens; I
reckon He gits somebody to help him. Don't
you, Aunt Minerva?"

CHAPTER VII

RABBITS' AND OTHER EGGS

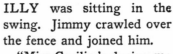ILLY was sitting in the swing. Jimmy crawled over the fence and joined him.

"Miss Cecilia 's dyeing me some Easter eggs," he said, "all blue and pink and green and yelluh and every kind they is; I tooken her some of our hen's eggs and she is going to fix 'em for me and they 'll be just like rabbit's eggs; I reckon I 'll have 'bout a million. I 'll give you one," he added generously.

"I want more 'n one," declared Billy, who was used to having the lion's share of everything.

"You all time talking 'bout you want more 'n one egg," said Jimmy. "You 'bout the stingiest Peter they is. Ain't you got no eggs? Get Miss Minerva to give you some of hers and I 'll take 'em over and

ask Miss Cecilia to dye 'em for you 'cause
you ain't 'quainted with her yet."

"Aunt Minerva ain't got none 'cep'in'
what she put under a ol' hen fer to set this
mornin'."

"Can't you get 'em from under the old
hen? Miss Minerva is such a Christian
woman, she ain't——"

"You done fool me 'bout that 'ligious business befo'," interrupted Billy, "an' I got put
to bed in the daytime."

"Well, she won't never miss two or three
eggs," coaxed Jimmy. "How many did she
put under the old hen?"

"She put fifteen," was the response, "an'
I don't believe she 'd want me to tech 'em."

"They 're 'bout the prettiest eggs ever
was," continued the tempter, "all blue and
pink and green, and 'bout a million kinds.
They 're just perzactly like rabbit's eggs."

"Me an' Wilkes Booth Lincoln ain't
never hear teller no rabbit's eggs since we 's
born," said Billy; "I don't berlieve rabbits
lays eggs nohow."

"They don' lay 'em 'cept to Easter," said
Jimmy. "Miss Cecilia 'splained it all to me
and she 's my Sunday-School teacher and
rabbits is bound to lay eggs 'cause it 's in

the Bible and she 's 'bout the prettiest
'splainer they is. I 'm going over there now
to see 'bout my eggs," and he made believe
to leave the swing.

"Le's us slip roun' to the hen-house an'
see what the ol' hen's a-doin'," suggested the
sorely tempted Billy. "Aunt Minerva is
a-makin' me some night-shirts an' she ain't
takin' no notice of nothin' else."

They tiptoed stealthily around the house
to the back-yard, but found the hen-house
door locked.

"Can't you get the key?" asked the
younger child.

"Naw, I can't," replied the other boy,
"but you can git in th'oo this-here little hole
what the chickens goes in at, whiles I
watches fer Aunt Minerva. I 'll stand right
here an' hol' my cap whiles you fetches me
the eggs. An' don't you take more 'n five
or six," he warned.

"I 'm skeered of the old hen," objected
Jimmy. "Is she much of a pecker?"

"Naw, she ain't a-goin' to hurt you," was
the encouraging reply. "Git up an' crawl
th'oo; I 'll help you."

Billy, having overcome his scruples, now

entered into the undertaking with great zest.

Jimmy climbed the chicken ladder, kicked his chubby legs through the aperture, hung suspended on his fat little middle for an instant, and finally, with much panting and tugging, wriggled his plump, round body into the hen-house. He walked over where a lonesome looking hen was sitting patiently on a nest. He put out a cautious hand and the hen promptly gave it a vicious peck.

"Billy," he called angrily, "you got to come in here and hold this old chicken; she's 'bout the terriblest pecker they is."

Billy stuck his head in the little square hole. "Go at her from behind," he suggested; "put yo' hand under her easy like, an' don' let her know what you 's up to."

Jimmy tried to follow these instructions, but received another peck for his pains. He promptly mutinied.

"If you want any eggs," he declared, scowling at the face framed in the aperture, "you can come get 'em yourself. I done monkeyed with this chicken all I 'm going to."

So Billy climbed up and easily got his lean

little body through the opening. He dex-
terously caught the hen by the nape of the
neck, as he had seen Aunt Cindy do, while
Jimmy reached for the eggs.

"If we ain't done lef' my cap outside on
the groun'," said Billy. "What we goin' to
put the eggs in?"

"Well, that's just like you, Billy, you all
time got to leave your cap on the ground.
I 'll put 'em in my blouse till you get outside and then I 'll hand 'em to you. How
many you going to take?"

"We might just as well git 'em all now,"
said Billy. "Aunt Cindy say they 's some
kinder hens won't lay no chickens 't all if
folks put they hands in they nests an' this
here hen look like to me she 's one of them
kind, so the rester the egg 'll jest be waste,
any how, 'cause you done put yo' han's in
her nes', an' a dominicker ain't a-goin' to
stan' no projeckin' with her eggs. Hurry
up."

Jimmy carefully distributed the eggs inside his blouse, and Billy once more crawled
through the hole and stood on the outside
waiting, cap in hand, to receive them.

But the patient hen had at last raised her
voice in angry protest and set up a furious

cackling, which so frightened the little boy
on the inside that he was panic-stricken.
He caught hold of a low roost pole, swung
himself up and, wholly unmindful of his

blouse full of eggs, pushed his lower limbs
through the hole and stuck fast. A pair of
chubby, sturdy legs, down which were

slowly trickling little yellow rivulets, and half of a plump, round body were all that would go through.

"Pull!" yelled the owner of the short fat legs. "I 'm stuck and can't go no furder. Pull me th'oo, Billy."

About this time the defrauded fowl flew from her nest and attempted to get out by her rightful exit. Finding it stopped up by a wriggling, squirming body she perched herself on the little boy's neck and flapped her enraged wings in his face.

"Pull!" yelled the child again, "help me th'oo, Billy, 'fore this fool chicken pecks all the meat off 'm my bones."

Billy grabbed the sticky limbs and gave a valiant tug, but the body did not move an inch. Alas, Jimmy with his cargo of broken eggs was fast imprisoned.

"Pull again!" yelled the scared and angry child, "you 'bout the idjetest idjet they is if you can't do no better 'n that."

Billy jerked with all his strength, but with no visible result.

"Pull harder! You no-count gump!" screamed the prisoner, beating off the hen with his hands.

The boy on the outside, who was strong

for his years, braced himself and gave a
mighty wrench of the other child's stout
extremities. Jimmy howled in pain and
gave his friend an energetic kick.

"Lemme go!" he shrieked, "you old im-
pe'dunt backbiter. I 'm going to tell Miss
Minerva you pulled my legs out by the
roots."

A small portion of the prisoner's blouse
was visible. Billy caught hold of it and
gave a strong jerk. There was a sound of
ripping and tearing and the older boy fell
sprawling on his back with a goodly portion
of the younger child's raiment in his hands.

"Now see what you done," yelled the victim of his energy, "you ain't got the sense of
a buffalo gnat. Oh! oh! This hole is 'bout
to cut my stomach open."

"Hush, Jimmy!" warned the other child.
"Don't make so much noise. Aunt Minerva
'll hear you."

"I want her to hear me," screamed Jimmy.
"You 'd like me to stay stuck in a chicken
hole all night. Oh! oh! oh!"

The noise did indeed bring Billy's aunt
out on a tour of investigation. She had to
knock a plank off the hen-house with an axe
before Jimmy's release could be accom-

plished. He was lifted down, red, angry, sticky, and perspiring, and was indeed a sight to behold.

"Billy got to all time perpose something to get little boys in trouble," he growled, "and got to all time get 'em stuck in a hole in a chicken-house."

"My nephew's name is William," corrected she.

"You perposed this here yo'self!" cried an indignant Billy. "Me an' Wilkes Booth Lincoln don' know nothin' 't all 'bout no rabbit's eggs sence we 's born."

"It does n't matter who proposed it," said his aunt firmly. "You are going to be punished, William. I have just finished one of your night-shirts. Come with me and put it on and go to bed. Jimmy, you go home and show yourself to your mother."

"Pick up yo' shirt-tail offer the groun' what I tore off, Jimmy," advised Billy, "an' take it home to yo' ma. Aunt Minerva," he pleaded, following mournfully behind her, "please don't put me to bed; the Major he don' go to bed no daytimes; I won't never get me no mo' eggs to make rabbit's eggs outer."

CHAPTER VIII

TELLERS OF TALES

THE days flew rapidly by. Miss Minerva usually attempted to train Billy all the morning, and by the mid-day dinner hour she was so exhausted that she was glad to let him play in the front yard during the afternoon.

Here he was often joined by the three children whose acquaintance he had made the day after his arrival, and the quartette became staunch friends and chums.

All four were sitting in the swing one warm spring day, under the surveillance of Billy's aunt, sewing on the veranda.

"Let 's tell tales," suggested Jimmy.

"All right," agreed Frances. "I 'll tell the first. Once there 's ——"

"Naw, you ain't neither," interrupted the little boy. "You all time talking 'bout you going to tell the first tale. I 'm going to tell the first tale myself. One time they 's ——"

"No, you are not either," said Lina positively. "Frances is a girl and she ought to be the first if she wants to. Don't you think so, Billy?"

"Yas, I does," championed he; "go on, Frances."

That little girl, thus encouraged, proceeded to tell the first tale:

"Once there 's a man named Mr. Elisha, and he had a friend named Mr. Elijah, so his mantelpiece fell on top of his head and make him perfectly bald; he has n't got a single hair and he has n't got any money, 'cause mama read me 'bout he rented his garments, which is clo'es, 'cause he did n't have none at all what belong to him. I s'pec' he just rented him a shirt and a pair o' breeches and wore 'em next to his hide 'thout no undershirt at all. He was drea'ful poor and had a miser'ble time and old mean Mr. Per'dventure took him up on a high mountain and left him, so when he come down some bad little childern say, 'Go 'long back, bald head!' and they make pock-mocks on him. Seems like everybody treat him bad, so he cuss 'em, so I never see anybody with a bald head 'thout I run, 'cause I don't want to get cussed. So two Teddy bears come out of the woods and ate up forty-two hunderd of 'em.''

"Why, Frances," reproved Lina, "you always get things wrong. I don't believe they ate up that many children."

"Yes, they did too," championed Jimmy, " 'cause it 's in the Bible and Miss Cecilia 'splained all 'bout it to me, and she's our Sunday-School teacher and 'bout the bullyest 'splainer they is. Them Teddy bears ate up 'bout a million chillens, which is all the little boys and girls two Teddy bears can hold at a time."

"I knows a man what ain't got no hair 't all on his head," remarked Billy; "he's a conjure-man an' me an' Wilkes Booth Lincoln been talkin' to him ever sence we 's born an' he ain't never cuss us, an' I ain't never got eat up by no Teddy bears neither. Huccome him to be bald? He's out in the fiel' one day a-pickin' cotton when he see a tu'key buzzard an' he talk to her like this:

" 'I say tu'key buzzard, I say,
    Who shall I see unexpected today?'

"If she flop her wings three times you goin' to see yo' sweetheart, but this-here buzzard ain't flop no wings 't all; she jes' lean over an' th'ow up on his head an' he been bald ever sence; ev'y single hair come out."

"Did you-all hear 'bout that 'Talian Dago that works on the section gang eating a buzzard?" asked Frances.

"Naw," said Billy. "Did it make him sick?"

"That it did," she answered; "he sent for Doctor Sanford and tells him, 'Me killa de big bird, me eat-a de big bird, de big bird make-a me seek.'"

"Them Dagoes 'bout the funniest talking folks they is," said Jimmy, "but they got to talk that way 'cause it 's in the Bible. They 'sputed on the tower of Babel and the Lord say 'Confound you!' Miss Cecilia 'splained it all to me and she 's 'bout the dandiest 'splainer they is."

"You may tell your tale now, Jimmy," said Lina.

"I 'm going to tell 'bout William Tell 'cause he 's in the Bible," said Jimmy. "Once they 's a man name'——"

"William Tell is n't in the Bible," declared Lina.

"Yes, he is too," contended the little boy, "Miss Cecilia 'splained it to me. You all

time setting yourself up to know more 'n
me and Miss Cecilia. One time they 's a
man name' William Tell and he had a little
boy what 's the cutest kid they is and the
Devil come 'long and temp' him. Then the
Lord say, 'William Tell, you and Adam and
Eve can taste everything they is in the garden 'cepting this one apple tree; you can get
all the pears and bunnanas and peaches and
grapes and oranges and plums and persim-
mons and scalybarks and fig leaves and 'bout
a million other kinds of fruit if you want
to, but don't you tech a single apple.' And
the Devil temp' him and say he going to
put his cap on a pole and everybody got
to bow down to it for a idol and if William
Tell don't bow down to it he got to shoot
a apple for good or evil off 'm his little boy's
head. That 's all the little boy William Tell
and Adam and Eve got, but he ain't going
to fall down and worship no gravy image
on top a pole, so he put a tomahawk in his
bosom and he tooken his bow and arruh and
shot the apple plumb th'oo the middle and
never swinge a hair of his head. And Eve
nibble off the apple and give Adam the core,
and Lina all time 'sputing 'bout Adam and

Eve and William Tell ain't in the Bible. They 're our first parents."

"Now, Billy, you tell a tale and then it will be my time," said Lina with a saving-the-best-for-the-last air.

"Once they was a ol' witch," said Billy, "what got outer her skin ev'y night an' lef' it on the he'rth an' turnt herself to a great, big, black cat an' go up the chim'ly an' go roun' an' ride folks fer horses, an' set on ev'ybody's chis' an' suck they breath an' kill 'em an' then come back to bed. An' can't nobody ketch her tell one night her husban' watch her an' he see her jump outer her skin an' drop it on the he'rth an' turn to a 'normous black cat an' go up the chim-'ly. An' he got outer the bed an' put some salt an' pepper an' vinegar on the skin an' she come back an' turnt to a 'oman an' try to git back in her skin an' she can't 'cause the salt an' pepper an' vinegar mos' burn her up, an' she keep on a-tryin' an' she can't never snuggle inter her skin 'cause it keep on a burnin' worser 'n ever, an' there she is a 'oman 'thout no skin on. So she try to turn back to a cat an' she can't 'cause it's pas' twelve erclock, an' she jest swivvle an' swiv-

vle tell fine'ly she jest swĭvvle all up. An'
that was the las' of the ole witch an' her
husban' live happy ever after. Amen."

"Once upon a time," said Lina, "there was
a beautiful maiden and she was in love, but
her wicked old parent wants her to marry a
rich old man threescore and ten years old,
which is 'most all the old you can get unless
you are going to die; and the lovely princess
said, 'No, father, you may cut me in the
twain but I will never marry any but my
true love.' So the wicked parent shut up
the lovely maiden in a high tower many
miles from the ground, and made her live on
turnips and she had nothing else to eat; so
one day when she was crying a little fairy
flew in at the window and asked, 'Why do
you weep, fair one?' And she said, 'A
wicked parent hath shut me up and I can't
ever see my lover any more.' So the fairy
touched her head with her wand and told
her to hang her hair out of the window, and
she did and it reached the ground, and her
lover, holding a rope ladder in one hand and
playing the guitar and singing with the
other, climbed up by her hair and took her
down on the ladder and his big black horse
was standing near, all booted and spurred,

and they rode away and lived happy ever after."

"How he goin' to clam' up, Lina," asked Billy, "with a rope ladder in one hand and his guitar in the other?"

"I don't know," was the dignified answer. "That is the way it is told in my fairy-tale book."

CHAPTER IX

CHANGING THE ETHIOPIAN

ILLY and Jimmy were sitting in the swing.

"What makes your hair curl just like a girl's?" asked the latter. "It's 'bout the curliest hair they is."

"Yes, it do," was Billy's mournful response. "It done worry me 'mos' to death. Ever sence me an' Wilkes Booth Lincoln's born we done try ev'ything fer to get the curl out. They was a Yankee man came 'long las' fall a-sellin' some stuff in a bottle what he call 'No-To-Kink' what he say would take the kink outer any nigger's head. An' Aunt Cindy bought a bottle fer to take the kink outer her hair an' me an' Wilkes Booth Lincoln put some on us heads an' it jes' make mine curlier 'n what it was already. I's 'shame' to go roun' folks with my cap off, a-lookin' like a frizzly chicken. Miss Cecilia say she like it though, an' we's en-

gaged. We's goin' to git married soon's
I puts on long pants."

"How long you been here, Billy?" asked
the other boy.

"Well, I don't know perxactly, but I been
to Sunday-School four times. I got engaged
to Miss Cecilia that very firs' Sunday, but
she did n' know it tell I went over to her
house the nex' day an' tol' her 'bout it. She
say she think my hair is so pretty."

"Pretty nothin'," sneered his rival. "She
jus' stuffin' you fuller 'n a tick with hot air.
It just makes you look like a girl. There's a
young lady come to spend a week with my
mama not long ago and she put somepin' on
her head to make it right yeller. She left
the bottle to our house and I know where 't
is. Maybe if you'd put some o' that on
your head 't would take the curl out."

" 'T ain't nothin' a-goin' to do it no good,"
gloomily replied Billy. " 'T would jest make
it yeller 'n what 't is now. Won't I be a
pretty sight when I puts on long pants with
these here yaller curls stuck on topper my
head? I'd 'nuther sight ruther be bal'-
headed."

"Bennie Dick 's got 'bout the kinkiest
head they is."

Bennie Dick was the two-year-old baby of Mrs. Garner's cook, Sarah Jane.

"It sho' is," replied Billy. Would n't he look funny if he had yaller hair, 'cause his face is so black?"

"I know where the bottle is," cried Jimmy, snatching eagerly at the suggestion. "Let's go get it and put some on Bennie Dick's head and see if it 'll turn it yeller."

"Aunt Minerva don' want me to go over to yo' house," objected Billy.

"You all time talking 'bout Miss Minerva won't let you go nowheres; she sure is imperdunt to you. You 'bout the 'fraidest boy they is. . . . Come on, Billy," pleaded Jimmy.

The little boy hesitated.

"I don't want to git Aunt Minerva's dander up any more 'n I jest natchelly boun' to," he said, following Jimmy reluctantly to the fence; "but I 'll jes' take a look at that bottle an' see ef it looks anything 't all like 'No-To-Kink'."

Giggling mightily, they jumped the dividing fence and slipped with stealthy tread around the house to Sarah Jane's cabin in the back-yard.

Bennie Dick was sitting on the floor before the open door, the entrance of which was securely barricaded to keep him inside. Sarah Jane was in the kitchen cooking supper; they could hear her happy voice raised in religious melody; Mrs. Garner had not yet returned from a card party; the coast was clear, and the time propitious.

Jimmy tiptoed to the house and soon returned with a big bottle of a powerful "blondine" in one hand and a stick of candy in the other.

"Bennie Dick," he said, "here 's a nice stick of candy for you if you 'll let us wash your head."

The negro baby's thick, red lips curved in a grin of delight, his shiny ebony face beamed happily, his round black eyes sparkled as he held out his fat, rusty little hands. He sucked greedily at the candy as the two mischievous little boys uncorked the bottle and poured a generous supply of the liquid on his head. They rubbed it in well, grinning with delight. They made a second and a third application before the bottle was exhausted; then they stood off to view the result of their efforts. The effect was ludicrous. The combination of coal black skin and red gold hair presented by the little

negro exceeded the wildest expectations of
Jimmy and Billy. They shrieked with
laughter and rolled over and over on the
floor in their unbounded delight.

"Hush!" warned Jimmy suddenly, "I believe Sarah Jane's coming out here to see
'bout Benny Dick. Let's get behind the
door and see what she's going to do."

> " 'Hit were good fer Paul an' Silas,
> Hit were good fer Paul an' Silas,
> Hit were good fer Paul an' Silas,
> An' hit's good ernough fer me.' "

floated Sarah Jane's song nearer and nearer.

> " 'Hit's de ole time erligion,
> Hit's de ole time' ——"

She caught sight of her baby with his
glistening black face and golden hair. She
threw up her hands, closed her eyes, and
uttered a terrified shriek. Presently she
slowly opened her eyes and took a second
peep at her curious-looking offspring. Sarah
Jane screamed aloud:

"Hit's de handiwork er de great Jehos-
haphat! Hit's de Marster's sign. Who
turnt yo' hair, Benny Dick?" she asked of

the sticky little pickaninny sitting happily on the floor. "Is a angel been here?"

Benny Dick nodded his head with a delighted grin of comprehension.

"Hit's de doing er de Lord," cried his mother. "He gwine turn my chile white an' he done begunt on his head!"

There was an ecstatic giggle from behind the door.

Sarah Jane rushed inside as fast as her mammoth proportions would admit and caught a culprit in each huge black paw.

"What yer up ter now, Jimmy Garner?" she asked. "What yer been er-doing?"

Sudden suspicion entered her mind as she caught sight of the empty bottle lying on a chair. "You been er-puttin' suthin' on my chile's head! I knows yer, I's er-gwine ter make yo' mammy gi' ye de worses' whippin' yer eber got an' I 's gwine ter take dis here William right ober ter Miss Minerva. Ain't y' all 'shame' er yerselves? Er tamperin' wid de ha'r what de good Lord put on er colored pusson's head an' er-tryin' fer ter scarify my feelin's like yer done. An' yer hear me, I 's gwine see dat somebody got ter scarify yer hides."

"If that ain't just like you, Billy," said

Jimmy, "you all time got to perpose to make nigger heads yeller and you all time getting little boys in trouble. You 'bout the smart Alexist jack-rabbit they is."

"You perposed this here hair business yo'self, Jimmy," retorted his fellow-conspirator. "You 's always blamin' yo' meanness on somebody else ever sence you 's born."

"Hit don't matter who perposed hit," said Sarah Jane firmly; "meanness has been did, an' y' all gotter be structified on de place pervided by natur fer ter lem my chile erlone."

CHAPTER X

LO! THE POOR INDIANS

ILLY had just decided to run down to the livery stable to pay Sam Lamb a visit when the gate opened, and Lina and Frances, their beloved dolls in their arms, came skipping in.

Jimmy, who had had a difference with Billy and was in the sulks on his own side of the fence, immediately crawled over and joined the others in the swing. He was lonesome and the prospect of companionship was too alluring for him to nurse his anger longer.

"Aunt Minerva 's gone to the Aid Society," remarked the host. "Don't y' all wish it met ev'y day 'stid 'er jes' meetin' ev'y Monday?"

"Yes, I do," agreed Frances, "you can have so much fun when our mamas go to the Aid. My mama 's gone too, so she left me with Brother and he 's writing a love letter to Ruth Shelton, so I slipped off."

"Mother has gone to the Aid, too," said Lina.

"My mama too," chimed in Jimmy, "she goes to the Aid every Monday and to card parties nearly all the time.   She told Sarah Jane to 'tend to me and Sarah Jane 's asleep. I hear her snoring. Ain't we glad there ain't no grown folks to meddle? Can't we have fun?"

"What 'll we play?" asked Frances, who had deliberately stepped in a mud puddle on the way, and splashed mud all over herself, "let 's make mud pies."

"Naw, we ain't a-going to make no mud pies," objected Jimmy.   "We can make mud pies all time when grown folks 'r' looking at you."

"Le's 's play sumpin' what we ain't never play, sence we 's born," put in Billy.

"I hope grandmother won't miss me." said Lina, "she 's reading a very interesting book."

"Let 's play Injun!" yelled Jimmy; "we ain't never play' Injun."

This suggestion was received with howls of delight.

"My mama 's got a box of red stuff that she puts on her face when she goes to the card parties. She never puts none on when she just goes to the Aid. I can run home and get the box to make us red like Injuns," said Frances.

"My mother has a box of paint, too."

"I ain't never see Aunt Minerva put no red stuff on her face," remarked Billy, disappointedly.

"Miss Minerva, she don't never let the Major come to see her, nor go to no card parties is the reason," explained the younger boy, "she just goes to the Aid where they ain't no men, and you don't hafter put no red on your face at the Aid. We 'll let you have some of our paint, Billy. My mama 's got 'bout a million diff'ent kinds."

"We got to have pipes," was Frances's next suggestion.

"My papa 's got 'bout a million pipes," boasted Jimmy, "but he got 'em all to the office, I spec'."

"Father has a meerschaum."

"Aunt Minerva ain't got no pipe."

"Miss Minerva 's 'bout the curiousest

woman they is," said Jimmy; "she ain't got nothing a tall; she ain't got no paint and she ain't got no pipe."

"Ladies don't use pipes, and we can do without them anyway," said Lina, "but we must have feathers; all Indians wear feathers."

"I 'll get my mama's duster," said Jimmy.

"Me, too," chimed in Frances.

Here Billy with flying colors came to the fore and redeemed Miss Minerva's waning reputation.

"Aunt Minerva 's got a great, big buncher tu'key feathers an' I can git 'em right now," and the little boy flew into the house and was back in a few seconds.

"We must have blankets, of course," said Lina, with the air of one whose word is law; "mother has a genuine Navajo."

"I got a little bow'narruh what Santa Claus bringed me," put in Jimmy.

"We can use hatchets for tomahawks," continued the little girl. "Come on, Frances; let us go home and get our things and come back here to dress up. Run, Jimmy, get your things! You, too, Billy!" she commanded.

The children ran breathlessly to their

homes nearby and collected the different ar-
ticles necessary to transform them into pre-
sentable Indians.

They soon returned, Jimmy dumping his
load over the fence and tumbling after; and
the happy quartette sat down on the grass
in Miss Minerva's yard. First the paint
boxes were opened and generously shared
with Billy, as with their handkerchiefs they
spread thick layers of rouge over their
charming, bright, mischievous little faces.

The feather decoration was next in order.

"How we goin' to make these feathers
stick?" asked Billy.

They were in a dilemma till the resource-
ful Jimmy came to the rescue.

"Wait a minute," he cried, "I'll be back
'fore you can say 'Jack Robinson'."

He rolled over the fence and was back in
a few minutes, gleefully holding up a bottle.

"This muc'lage 'll make 'em stick," he
panted, almost out of breath.

Lina assumed charge of the head-dresses.
She took Billy first, rubbed the mucilage
well into his sunny curls, and filled his
head full of his aunt's turkey feathers, leaving them to stick out awkwardly in all direc-
tions and at all angles. Jimmy and Frances,

after robbing their mothers' dusters, were similarly decorated, and last, Lina, herself, was tastefully arrayed by the combined efforts of the other three.

At last all was in readiness.

Billy, regardless of consequences, had

pinned his aunt's newest grey blanket around him and was viewing, with satis-fied admiration, its long length trailing on the grass behind him; Lina had her mother's treasured Navajo blanket draped around her graceful little figure; Frances, after pulling the covers off of several beds and finding nothing to suit her fanciful taste, had snatched a gorgeous silk afghan from the leather couch in the library. It was an expensive affair of intricate pattern, delicate stitches, and beautiful embroidery with a purple velvet border and a yellow satin lining. She had dragged one corner of it through the mud puddle and torn a big rent in another place.

Jimmy was glorious in a bright red blanket, carrying his little bow and arrow.

"I'm going to be the Injun chief," he boasted.

"I'm going to be a Injun chief, too," parroted Frances.

"Chief, nothing!" he sneered, "you all time trying to be a Injun chief. You 'bout the pompousest little girl they is. You can't be a chief nohow; you got to be a squash, Injun ladies 'r' name' squashes; me an' Billy's the chiefs. I'm name' old Setting Bull, hi'self."

"You can't be named 'Bull,' Jimmy," reproved Lina, "it is n't genteel to say 'bull' before people."

"Yes, I am too," he contended. "Setting

Bull 's the biggest chief they is and I 'm
going to be name' him."

"Well, I am not going to play then," said
Lina primly, "my mother wants me to be
genteel, and 'bull' is not genteel."

"I tell you what, Jimmy," proposed Frances, "you be name' 'Setting Cow.' 'Cow' is
genteel 'cause folks milk 'em."

"Naw, I ain't going to be name' no cow,
neither," retorted the little Indian, "you all
time trying to 'suade somebody to be name'
'Setting Cow'."

"He can't be name' a cow,"—Billy now
entered into the discussion —" 'cause he ain't
no girl. Why don' you be name' 'Settin'
Steer'? Is 'steer' genteel, Lina?" he anxiously inquired.

"Yes, he can be named 'Sitting Steer',"
she granted. Jimmy agreeing to the compromise, peace was once more restored.

"Frances and Lina got to be the squashes
——" he began.

"It is n't 'squashes,' it is 'squaws,' " corrected Lina.

"Yes, 't is squashes too," persisted Jimmy,
" 'cause it 's in the Bible and Miss Cecilia
'splained it to me and she's 'bout the high-
steppingest 'splainer they is. Me and Billy

is the chiefs," he shouted, capering around, "and you and Frances is the squashes and got to have papooses strop' to your back."

"Bennie Dick can be a papoose," suggested Billy.

"I 'm not going to be a Injun squash if I got to have a nigger papoose strapped to my back!" cried an indignant Frances. "You can strap him to your own back, Billy."

"But I ain't no squash," objected that little Indian.

"We can have our dolls for papooses," said Lina, going to the swing where the dolls had been left. Billy pulled a piece of string from his pocket and the babies were safely strapped to their mothers' backs. With stately tread, headed by Sitting Steer, the children marched back and forth across the lawn in Indian file.

So absorbed were they in playing Indian that they forgot the flight of time until their chief suddenly stopped, all his brave valor gone as he pointed with trembling finger up the street.

That part of the Ladies' Aid Society which lived in West Covington was bearing down upon them.

"Yonder 's our mamas and Miss Minerva,"

he whispered. "Now look what a mess
Billy's done got us in; he all time got to
perpose someping to get chillens in trouble
and he all time got to let grown folks ketch
'em."

"Are n't you ashamed to tell such a story,
Jimmy Garner?" cried Frances. "Billy did
n't propose any such thing. Come on, let 's
run," she suggested.

" 'T ain't no use to run," advised Jimmy.
"They 're too close and done already see us.
We boun' to get what 's coming to us anyway, so you might jus' as well make 'em
think you ain't 'fraid of 'em. Grown folks
got to all time think little boys and girls 'r'
skeered of 'em, anyhow."

"Aunt Minerva 'll sho' put me to bed this
time," said Billy. "Look like ev'y day I
gotter go to bed."

"Mother will make me study the catechism all day to-morrow," said Lina dis-
mally.

"Mama 'll lock me up in the little closet
under the stairway," said Frances.

"My mama 'll gimme 'bout a million licks
and try to take all the hide off o' me," said
Jimmy; "but we done had a heap of fun."

It was some hours later. Billy's aunt had

ruthlessly clipped the turkey feathers from his head, taking the hair off in great patches. She had then boiled his scalp, so the little boy thought, in her efforts to remove the mucilage. Now, shorn of his locks and of some of his courage, the child was sitting quietly by her side, listening to a superior moral lecture and indulging in a compulsory heart-to-heart talk with his relative.

"I don't see that it does you any good, William, to put you to bed."

"I don' see as it do neither," agreed Billy.

"I can not whip you; I am constitutionally opposed to corporal punishment for children."

"I 's 'posed to it too," he assented.

"I believe I will hire a servant, so that I may devote my entire time to your training."

This prospect for the future did not appeal to her nephew. On the contrary it filled him with alarm.

"A husban' 'd be another sight handier," he declared with energy; "he 'd be a heap mo' 'count to you 'n a cook, Aunt Minerva. There 's that Major ——"

"You will never make a preacher of yourself, William, unless you improve."

The child looked up at her in astonishment; this was the first he knew of his being destined for the ministry.

"A preacher what 'zorts an' calls up mourners?" he said, — "not on yo' tin-type. Me an' Wilkes Booth Lincoln —"

"How many times have I expressed the wish not to have you bring that negro's name into the conversation?" she impatiently interrupted.

"I don' perzactly know, 'm," he answered good humoredly, " 'bout fifty hunerd, I reckon. Anyways, Aunt Minerva, I ain't goin' to be no preacher. When I puts on long pants I 's goin' to be a Confedrit Vet'run an' kill 'bout fifty hunderd Yankees an' Injuns, like my Major man."

CHAPTER XI

NOW RIDDLE ME THIS

HE children were sitting in the swing. Florence Hammer, a little girl whose mother was spending the day at Miss Minerva's, was with them.

"Don't you-all wish Santa Claus had his birthday right now 'stead 'o waiting till Christmas to hang up our stockings?" asked Frances.

"Christmas is n't Santa Claus' birthday," corrected Lina. "God was born on Christmas and that 's the reason we hang up our stockings."

"Yes; it is old Santa's birthday, too," argued Jimmy, "'cause it 's in the Bible and Miss Cecilia 'splained it to me and she 'bout the dandiest 'splainer they is."

"Which you-all like the best: God or Doctor Sanford or Santa Claus?" asked Florence.

"I like God 'nother sight better 'n I do anybody," declared Jimmy, "'cause He so forgivingsome. He's 'bout the forgivingest person they is. Santa Claus can't let you go to Heaven nor Doctor Sanford neither, nor our papas and mamas nor Miss Minerva. Now would n't we be in a pretty fix if we had to 'pend on Doctor Sanford or Santa Claus to forgive you every time you run off or fall down and bust your breeches. Naw; gimme God ev'y time."

"I like Santa Claus the best," declared Frances, "'cause he is n't f'rever getting in your way, and has n't any castor oil like Doctor Sanford, and you don't f'rever have to be telling him you 're sorry you did what you did, and he has n't all time got one eye on you either, like God, and got to follow you 'round. And Santa Claus don't all time say, 'Shet your eyes and open your mouth,' like Doctor Sanford, 'and poke out your tongue.'"

"I like Doctor Sanford the best," said Florence, "'cause he 's my uncle, and God and Santa Claus ain't kin to me."

"And the Bible say, 'Love your kin-folks,' Miss Cecilia 'splained —"

"I use to like my Uncle Doc' heap bet-

ter 'n what I do now," went on the little
girl, heedless of Jimmy's interruption, "till
I went with daddy to his office one day.
And what you reckon that man 's got in his
office? He 'is got a dead man 'thout no
meat nor clo'es on, nothing a tall but just
his bones."

"Was he a hant?" asked Billy. "I like
the Major best — he 's got meat on."

"Naw; he did n't have no sheet on — just
bones," was the reply.

"No sheet on; no meat on!" chirruped
Billy, glad of the rhyme.

"Was he a angel, Florence?" questioned
Frances.

"Naw; he did n't
have no harp and no
wings neither."

"It must have been
a skeleton," explained
Lina.

"And Uncle Doc'
just keeps that poor
man there and won't
let him go to Heaven
where d e a d f o l k s
b'longs."

"I spec' he was n't

a good man 'fore he died and got to go to
the Bad Place," suggested Frances.

"I 'll betcher he never asked God to forgive him when he 'ceived his papa and
sassed his mama,"— this from Jimmy,—
"and Doctor Sanford 's just a-keeping old
Satan from getting him to toast on a pitchfork."

"I hope they 'll have a Christmas tree
at Sunday-School next Christmas," said
Frances, harking back, "and I hope I 'll get
a heap o' things like I did last Christmas.
Poor little Tommy Knott he 's so skeered
he was n't going to get nothing at all on the
tree so he got him a great, big, red apple
an' he wrote on a piece o' paper 'From
Tommy Knott to Tommy Knott,' and tied it
to the apple and put it on the tree for
hi'self."

"Let 's ask riddles," suggested Lina.

"All right," shouted Frances, "I 'm going
to ask the first."

"Naw; you ain't neither," objected Jimmy.
"You all time got to ask the first riddle.
I 'm going to ask the first one —

" 'Round as a biscuit, busy as a bee,

Prettiest little thing you ever did see?'——

'A watch.'

' 'Humpty Dumpty set on a wall,
    Humpty Dumpty had a great fall,
    All the king's horses and all the king's
        men
    Can't put Humpty Dumpty back again.'
                       'A egg.'

" 'Round as a ring, deep as a cup,
    All the king's horses can't pull it up.'
                     'A well.'

" 'House full, yard full, can't ketch ——' "

"Hush, Jimmy!" cried Lina, in disgust. "You don't know how to ask riddles. You must n't give the answers, too. Ask one riddle at a time and let some one else answer it. I 'll ask one and see who can answer it:

" 'As I was going through a field of wheat
    I picked up something good to eat,
    'T was neither fish nor flesh nor bone,
    I kept it till it ran alone?' "

"A snake! A snake!" guessed Florence. "That 's a easy riddle."

"Snake, nothing!" scoffed Jimmy, "you can't eat a snake. 'Sides Lina would n't 'a' picked up a snake. Is it a little baby rabbit, Lina?"

"It was neither fish nor flesh nor bone,"

she declared; "and a rabbit is flesh and bone."

"Then it 's boun' to be a apple," was Jimmy's next guess; "that ain't no flesh and blood and it 's good to eat."

"An apple can't run alone," she triumphantly answered. "Give it up? Well, it was an egg and it hatched to a chicken. Now, Florence, you ask one."

"S'pose a man was locked up in a house," she asked, "how 'd he get out?"

"Clam' outer a winder," guessed Billy.

" 'T wa'n't no winder to the house," she declared.

"Crawled out th'oo the chim'ly, like Santa Claus," was Billy's next guess.

" 'T wa'n't no chim'ly to it. Give it up? Give it up?" the little girl laughed gleefully. "Well, he just broke out with measles."

"It is Billy's time," said Lina, who seemed to be mistress of ceremonies.

"Tabernicle learnt this here one at school; see, if y' all can guess it: 'Tabby had four kittens but Stillshee did n't have none 't all' "

"I don't see no sense a tall in that," argued Jimmy, " 'thout some bad little boys drownded 'em."

"Tabby was a cat," explained the other

boy, "and she had four kittens; and Stillshee was a little girl, and she did n't have no kittens 't all."

"What 's this," asked Jimmy: " 'A man rode 'cross a bridge and Fido walked?' Had a little dog name' Fido."

"You did n't ask that right, Jimmy," said Lina, "you always get things wrong. The riddle is, 'A man rode across a bridge and Yet he walked,' and the answer is, 'He had a little dog named Yet who walked across the bridge.' "

"Well, I 'd 'nother sight ruther have a little dog name' Fido," declared Jimmy. "A little dog name' Yet and a little girl name' Stillshee ain't got no sense a tall to it."

"Why should a hangman wear suspenders?" asked Lina. "I 'll bet nobody can answer that."

"To keep his breeches from falling off," triumphantly answered Frances.

"No, you goose, a hangman should wear suspenders so that he 'd always have a gallows handy."

CHAPTER XII

IN THE HOUSE OF THE LORD.

I T was a beautiful Sunday morning.

The pulpit of the Methodist Church was not occupied by its regular pastor, Brother Johnson. Instead, a traveling minister, collecting funds for a church orphanage in Memphis, was the speaker for the day. Miss Minerva rarely missed a service in her own church. She was always on hand at the Love Feast and the Missionary Rally and gave liberally of her means to every cause. She was sitting in her own pew between Billy and Jimmy, Mr. and Mrs. Garner having remained at home. Across the aisle from her sat Frances Black, between her father and mother; two pews in front of her were Mr. and Mrs. Hamilton, with Lina on the outside next the aisle. The good Major was there, too; it was the only place he could depend upon for seeing Miss Minerva.

The preacher, after an earnest and eloquent discourse from the text, "He will remember the fatherless," closed the big Bible with a bang calculated to wake any who might be sleeping. He came down from the pulpit and stood close to his hearers as he made his last pathetic appeal.

"My own heart," said he, "goes out to every orphan child, for in the yellow fever epidemic of '78, when but two years old, I lost both father and mother. If there are any little orphan children here to-day, I should be glad if they would come up to the front and shake hands with me."

Now Miss Minerva always faithfully responded to every proposal made by a preacher; it was a part of her religious conviction. At revivals she was ever a shining, if solemn and austere, light. When a minister called for all those who wanted to go to Heaven to rise, she was always the first one on her feet. If he asked to see the raised hands of those who were members of the church at the tender age of ten years, Miss Minerva's thin, long arm gave a prompt response. Once when a celebrated evangelist was holding a big protracted meeting under canvas in the town and had

asked all those who had read the book of
Hezekiah in the Bible to stand up, Miss
Minerva on one side of the big tent and her
devoted lover on the other side were among
the few who had risen to their feet. She
had read the good book from cover to cover
from Genesis to Revelation over and over
so she thought she had read Hezekiah a
score of times.

So now, when the preacher called for
little orphans to come forward, she leaned
down and whispered to her nephew, "Go
up to the front, William, and shake hands
with the nice kind preacher."

"Wha' fer?" he asked. "I don' want to
go up there; ev'ybody here 'll look right at
me."

"Are there no little orphans here?" the
minister was saying. "I want to shake the
hand of any little child who has had the
misfortune to lose its parents."

"Go on, William," commanded his aunt.
"Go shake hands with the preacher."

The little boy again demurred but, Miss
Minerva insisting, he obediently slipped by
her and by his chum. Walking gracefully
and jauntily up the aisle to the spot where

the lecturer was standing by a broad table, he held out his slim, little hand.

Jimmy looked at these proceedings of Billy's in astonishment, not comprehending at all. He was rather indignant that the older boy had not confided in him and invited his participation.

But Jimmy was not the one to sit calmly by and be ignored when there was anything doing, so he slid awkwardly from the bench before Miss Minerva knew what he was up to. Signaling Frances to follow, he swaggered pompously behind Billy and he, too, held out a short, fat hand to the minister.

The speaker smiled benignly down upon them; lifting them up in his arms he stood the little boys upon the table. He thought the touching sight of these innocent and tender little orphans would empty the pockets of the audience. Billy turned red with embarrassment at his conspicuous position, while Jimmy grinned happily at the amused congregation. Horrified Miss Minerva half rose to her feet, but decided to remain where she was. She was a timid woman and did not know what course she ought to pursue. Besides, she had just caught the Major's smile.

"And how long have you been an orphan?" the preacher was asking of Billy.

"Ever sence me an' Wilkes Booth Lincoln 's born," sweetly responded the child.

"I 'bout the orphantest boy they is," volunteered Jimmy.

Frances, responding to the latter's invitation, had crawled over her father's legs before he realized what was happening. She, too, went sailing down the aisle, her stiff white dress standing straight up in the back like a strutting gobbler's tail. She grabbed hold of the man's hand, and was promptly lifted to the table beside the other "orphans." Tears stood in the good preacher's eyes as he turned to the tittering audience and said in a pathetic voice, "Think of it, my friends, this beautiful little girl has no mother."

Poor Mrs. Black! A hundred pairs of eyes sought her pew and focused themselves upon the pretty young woman sitting there, red, angry, and shamefaced. Mr. Black was visibly amused and could hardly keep from laughing aloud.

As Frances passed by the Hamiltons' pew in her promenade down the aisle, Mrs. Hamilton leaned across her husband and made an attempt to clutch Lina; but she was too late; already that dignified little "orphan" was gliding with stately, conscious tread to join the others. This was too much for the audience. A few boys laughed out and for the first time the preacher's suspicions were aroused. As he clasped Lina's slender, graceful little hand he asked:

"And you have no father or mother, little girl?"

"Yes, I have, too," she angrily retorted.
"My father and mother are sitting right
there," and she pointed a slim forefinger to
her crimson, embarrassed parents.

CHAPTER XIII

JOB AND POLLIE BUMPUS

NEVER have told a down-right falsehood," said Lina. "Mother taught me how wicked it is to tell stories. Did you ever tell a fib to your mother, Frances?"

" 'T ain't no use to try to 'ceive my mama," was the reply of the other little girl; "she 's got such gimlet eyes and ears she can tell with 'em shut if you 're fibbing. I gave up hope long ago, so I just go 'long and tell her the plain gospel truth when she asks me, 'cause I know those gimlet eyes and ears of hers 're going to worm it out o' me somehow."

"Grown folks pin you down so close sometimes," said Jimmy, "you bound to 'varicate a little; and I always tell God I 'm sorry. I tell my mama the truth 'most all time 'cepting when she asks questions 'bout things ain't none of her business a tall, and she all time want to know 'Who done it?' and if I let on it 's me, I know she 'll wear out all the slippers and hair-brushes they is paddling my canoe, 'sides switches, so I jus' say 'I do' know, 'm'—which all time ain't perzactly the truth. You ever tell Miss Minerva stories, Billy?"

"Aunt Cindy always say, 't wa'n't no harm 't all to beat 'bout the bush an' try to th'ow folks offer the track 'long as you can, but if it come to the point where you got to tell a out-an'-out fib, she say for me always to tell the truth, an' I jest nachelly do like she say ever sence I 's born," replied Billy.

The children swung awhile in silence. Presently Jimmy broke the quiet by remarking:

"Don't you all feel sorry for old Miss Pollie Bumpus? She live all by herself, and she 'bout a million years old, and Doctor Sanford ain't never brung her no chillens 'cause she ain't got 'er no husban' to be their papa, and she got a octopus in her head, and she poor as a post and deaf as Job's old turkey-hen."

"Job's old turkey-hen was n't deaf," retorted Lina primly; "she was very, very poor and thin."

"She was deaf, too," insisted Jimmy, "'cause it's in the Bible. I know all 'bout Job," bragged he.

"I know all 'bout Job, too," chirped Frances.

"Job, nothing!" said Jimmy, with a sneer; "you all time talking 'bout you know all 'bout Job; you 'bout the womanishest little girl they is. Now I know Job 'cause Miss Cecilia 'splained all 'bout him to me. He's in the Bible and he sold his birthmark for a mess of potatoes and——"

"You never can get anything right, Jimmy," interrupted Lina; "that was Esau and it was not his birthmark, it was his birthstone; and he sold his birthstone for a mess of potash."

"Yas," agreed Frances; "'he saw Esau kissing Kate and Esau had to sell him his birthstone to keep his mouth shut."

"Mother read me all about Job," continued Lina; "he was afflicted with boils and his wife knit him a Job's comforter to wrap around him, and he ——"

"And he sat under a 'tato vine," put in Frances eagerly, "what God grew to keep the sun off o' his boils and ——"

"That was Jonah," said Lina, "and it was n't a potato vine; it was ——"

"No, 't was n't Jonah neither; Jonah is inside of a whale's bel ——"

"Frances!"

"Stommick," Frances corrected herself, "and a whale swallow him, and how 's he going to sit under a pumpkin vine when he 's inside of a whale?"

"It was not a pumpkin vine, it ——"

"And I 'd jus' like to see a man inside of a whale a-setting under a morning-glory vine."

"The whale vomicked him up," said Jimmy.

"What sorter thing is a octopus like what y' all say is in Miss Pollie Bumpus's head?" asked Billy.

"'T ain't a octopus, it 's a polypus," explained Frances, "'cause she 's named Miss Pollie. It 's a someping that grows in your nose and has to be named what you 's named. She 's named Miss Pollie and she 's got a polypus."

"I 'm mighty glad my mama ain't got no Eva-pus in her head," was Jimmy's comment. "Ain't you glad, Billy, your Aunt Minerva ain't got no Miss Minerva-pus?"

"I sho' is," fervently replied Miss Minerva's nephew; "she 's hard 'nough to manage now like she is."

"I'm awful good to Miss Pollie," said Frances. "I take her someping good to eat 'most every day. I took her two pieces of pie this morning; I ate up one piece on the way and she gimme the other piece when I got there. I jus' don't believe she could get 'long at all 'thout me to carry her the good things to eat that my mama sends her; I takes her pies all the time; she says they 're the best smelling pies ever she smelt."

"You 'bout the piggiest girl they is," said Jimmy, "all time got to eat up a poor old woman's pies. You'll have a Frances-pus in your stomach first thing you know."

"She 's got a horn that you talk th'oo," continued the little girl, serenely contemptuous of Jimmy's adverse criticism, "and 'fore I knew how you talk into it, she says to me one day, 'How 's your ma?' and stuck that old horn at me; so I put it to my ear, too, and there we set; she got one end of the horn to her ear and I got the other end to my ear; so when I saw this was n't going to work I took it and blew into it; you-all 'd died a-laughing to see the way I did. But now I can talk th'oo it 's good 's anybody."

"That is an ear trumpet, Frances," said Lina, "it is not a horn."

"Le's play 'Hide the Switch,'" suggested Billy.

"I 'm going to hide it first," cried Frances.

"Naw, you ain't," objected Jimmy, "you all time got to hide the switch first. I 'm going to hide it first myself."

"No, I 'm going to say 'William Com Trimbleton,'" said Frances, "and see who 's going to hide it first. Now you-all spraddle out your fingers."

CHAPTER XIV.

MR. ALGERNON JONES

GAIN was it Monday, with the Ladies Aid Society in session. Jimmy was sitting on the grass in his own front yard, in full view of Sarah Jane, who was ironing clothes in her cabin with strict orders to keep him at home. Billy was in the swing in Miss Minerva's yard.

"Come on over," he invited.

"I can't," was the reply across the fence, "I 'm so good now I 'bout got 'ligion; I reckon I 'm going to be a mish'nary or a pol'tician, one or t' other when I 'm a grown-up man 'cause I 'm so good; I ain't got but five whippings this week. I been good ever since I let you 'suade me to play Injun. I 'm the goodest little boy in this town, I 'spec'. Sometimes I get scared 'bout being so good 'cause I hear a woman say if you too good, you going to die or you ain't got no sense, one. You come on over here; you ain't trying to be good like what I'm trying, and Miss Minerva don't never do nothing a tall to you 'cepting put you to bed."

"I 'd ruther to git whipped fifty hunderd times 'n to hafter go to bed in the daytime with Aunt Minerva lookin' at you. An' her specs can see right th'oo you plumb to the bone. Naw, I can't come over there 'cause she made me promise not to. I ain't never go back on my word yit."

"I hope mama won't never ask me to promise her nothing a tall, 'cause I 'm mighty curious 'bout forgetting. I 'spec' I 'm the most forgettingest little boy they is. But I 'm so glad I 'm so good. I ain't never going to be bad no more; so you might just as well quit begging me to come over and swing, you need n't ask me no more, — 't ain't no use a tall."

"I ain't a-begging you," cried Billy contemptuously, "you can set on yo' mammy's grass where you is, an' be good from now tell Jedgement Day an' 't won't make no change in my business."

"I ain't going to be 'ticed into no meanness, 'cause I 'm so good," continued the reformed one, after a short silence during which he had seen Sarah Jane turn her back to him, "but I don't b'lieve it 'll be no harm jus' to come over and set in the swing with you; maybe I can 'fluence you to be good like me and keep you from 'ticing little boys into mischief. I think I 'll just come over and set a while and help you to be good," and he started to the fence. Sarah Jane turned around in time to frustrate his plans.

"You git right back, Jimmy," she yelled, "you git erway f'om dat-ar fence an' quit confabbin' wid dat-ar Willyum. Fixin' to make some mo' Injuns out o' yo'selfs, ain't yeh, or some yuther kin' o' skeercrows?"

Billy strolled to the other side of the big yard and climbed up and sat on the tall gate post. A stranger, coming from the opposite direction, stopped and spoke to him.

"Does Mr. John Smith live here?" he asked.

"Naw, sir," was the reply; "don't no Mr. 't all live here; jest me an' Aunt Minerva, an' she turns up her nose at anything that wears pants."

"And where could I find your Aunt Minerva?" the stranger's grin was ingratiating and agreeable.

"Why, this here 's Monday," the little boy exclaimed. "Of course she 's at the

Aid; all the 'omans roun' here goes to the
Aid on Monday."

"Your aunt is an old friend of mine," went
on the man, "and I knew she was at the
Aid. I just wanted to find out if you'd tell
the truth about her. Some little boys tell
stories, but I am glad to find out you are so
truthful. My name is Mr. Algernon Jones
and I'm glad to know you. Shake! Put
it there, partner," and the fascinating
stranger held out a grimy paw.

Billy smiled down from his perch at him
and thought he had never met such a pleas-
ant man. If he was such an old friend of
his aunt's maybe she would not object to
him because he wore pants, he thought.
Maybe she might be persuaded to take Mr.
Jones for a husband. Billy almost hoped
that she would hurry home from the Aid,
he wanted to see the two together so.

"Is you much of a cusser?" he asked sol-
emnly, " 'cause if you is you'll hafter cut it
out on these premises."

Mr. Jones seemed much surprised and
hurt at the question.

"An oath never passed these lips," replied
the truthful gentleman.

"Can you churn?"

"Churn — churn?" with a reminiscent smile, "I can churn like a top."

Jimmy was dying of curiosity but the gate was too far away for him to do more than catch a word now and then. It was also out of Sarah Jane's visual line, so she knew nothing of the stranger's advent.

"And you 're here all by yourself?" insinuated Billy's new friend. "And the folks next door, where are they?"

"Mrs. Garner 's at the Aid an' Mr. Garner 's gone to Memphis. That is they little boy a-settin' in they yard on they grass," answered the child.

"I 've come to fix your Aunt Minerva's water pipe," said truth-loving Mr. Jones. "Come, show me the way; I'm the plumber."

"In the bath-room?" asked the child. "I did n' know it needed no fixin'."

He led the agreeable plumber through the hall, down the long back-porch to the bath-room, remarking:

"I 'll jes' watch you work." And he seated himself in the only chair.

Here is where Billy received one of the greatest surprises of his life. The fascinating stranger grabbed him with a rough hand and hissed:

"Don't you dare open your mouth or I 'll crack your head open and scatter your brains. I 'll eat you alive."

The fierce, bloodshot eyes, which had seemed so laughing and merry before, now glared into those of the little boy as the man took a stout cord from his pocket, bound Billy to the chair, and gagged him with a large bath towel. Energetic Mr. Jones took the key out of the door, shook his fist at the child, went out, and locked the door behind him.

Jimmy, seeing no hope of eluding Sarah Jane's vigilance, resorted to strategy and deceit.

" 'T ain't no fun setting out here," he called to her, "so I 'm going in the house and take a nap."

She willingly consented, as she was through with her ironing and thought to snatch a few winks of sleep herself.

The little boy slipped quietly through the house, noiselessly across the back-yard and into his father's big garden, which was sepa-rated from that of his neighbor by a high board-fence. He quickly climbed the fence, flew across Miss Minerva's tomato patch and tiptoed up her back steps to the back-porch, his little bare feet giving no sign of his presence. Hearing curious noises coming from the bath-room, where Billy was bumping the chair up and down in his efforts to release his mouth, he made for that spot, promptly unlocked the door, and walked in. Billy by scuffling and tugging had freed his mouth from the towel that bound it at that moment.

"Hush!" he whispered as Jimmy opened the door, "you 'll get eat up alive if you don't look out." His tone was so mysterious and thrilling and he looked so scared tied to the chair that the younger boy's blood almost froze in his veins.

"What you doing all tied up so?" he asked in low, frightened tones.

"Mr. Algernon Jones done it. I spec' he 's a robber an' is jes' a-robberin' right now," answered Billy.

"I 'll untie you," said his chum.

"Naw; you better not," said Billy bravely. "He might git away. You leave me jes' like he fixed me so 's you can try to ketch him. I hear him in the dinin'-room now. You leave me right here an' step over to yo' house an' 'phone to some mens to come and

git him quick. Shet the do' ag'in an' don't
make no noise. Fly, now!"

And Jimmy did fly. He again took the
garden route and in a minute was at the
telephone with the receiver at his ear.

"Hello! Is that you, Miss Central? This
is me," he howled into the transmitter.
"Gimme Miss Minerva's beau. I don't know
his number, but he 's got a office over my
papa's bank."

His father being out of town, the little boy
shrewdly decided that Miss Minerva's beau
was the next best man to help capture the
robber.

"Miss Minerva what lives by me," he
shrieked.

Fortunately Central recognized his childish voice and was willing to humor him, so
as she too knew Miss Minerva's beau the
connection was quickly made.

"Hello! Is that you, Major? This is me.
If you don't want Mr. Algernon Jones to
be robbering everything Miss Minerva 's got
you better get a move on and come right
this minute. You got to hustle and bring
'bout a million pistols and guns and swords
and tomahawks and all the mans you can
find and dogs. He 's the fiercest robber ever

was, and he 's already done tie Billy to a
bath-room chair and done eat up 'bout a
million cold biscuits, I spec'. All of us is
'bout to be slewed. Good-bye."

The plump, round gentleman at the other
end of the wire heard this amazing message
in the utmost confusion and consternation.
He frantically rang the telephone again and
again but could get no answer from the
Garners' home so he put on his hat and
walked the short distance to Miss Minerva's
house.

Jimmy was waiting to receive him at the
front gate, having again eluded Sarah Jane's
vigilance.

"Hush!" he whispered mysteriously, "he 's
in the dining-room. Ain't you bringed nobody else? Get your pistol and come on."

Mr. Algernon Jones, feeling safe and
secure for the next hour and having par-
taken of a light lunch, was in the act of
transferring some silver spoons from the
sideboard to his pockets when a noise at the
dining-room door caused him to look in that
direction. With an oath he sprang forward,
and landed his fist upon the nose of a plump
gentleman standing there, bringing a stream
of blood and sending him sprawling to the

floor. Mr. Jones overturned a big-eyed little
boy who was in his way and, walking rapidly
in the direction of the railroad, the erstwhile
plumber was seen no more.

Jimmy quickly recovered himself and
sprang to his feet. Seeing the blood stream-
ing down the white shirt front of Miss
Minerva's unconscious beau, he gathered his
wits together and took the thread of events

again into his own little hands. He flung himself over the fence, careless of Sarah Jane this time, mounted a chair and once more rang the telephone.

"Hello! Is that you, Miss Central? This is me some more. Gimme Doctor Sanford's office, please."

"Hello! Is that you, Doctor? This is me. Mr. Algernon Jones done kilt Miss Minerva's beau. He's on her back-porch bloody all over. He's 'bout the deadest man they is. You'd better come toreckly you can and bring the hearse, and a coffin and a clean shirt and a tombstone. He's wounded me but I ain't dead yet. Good-bye."

Doctor Sanford received Jimmy's crazy message in astonishment. He, too, rang the telephone again and again but could hear nothing more, so he walked down to Miss Minerva's house and rang the door-bell. Jimmy opened the door and led the way to the back-porch, where the injured man, who had just recovered consciousness, was sitting limply in a chair.

"What does all this mean? Are you hurt?" asked the Doctor as he examined Mr. Jones's victim.

"No, I think I'm all right now," was the

reply; "but that scoundrel certainly gave me a severe blow."

Billy, shut up in the bath-room and listening to all the noise and confusion, had been scared nearly out of his senses. He had kept as still as a mouse till now, when, thinking he heard friendly voices he yelled out, "Open the do' an' untie me."

"We done forgot Billy," said the little rescuer, as he ran to the bath-room door and opened it. He was followed by the Doctor, who cut the cords that bound the prisoner.

"Now, William," commanded Doctor Sanford as they grouped themselves around the stout, plump gentleman in the chair, "begin at the beginning, and let us get at the bottom of this affair."

"Mr. Algernon Jones he come to the gate," explained the little boy, "an' he say he goin' to fix the water pipe an' he say he 's a plumber. He 's a very 'greeable man, but I don't want Aunt Minerva to marry him, now. I was plumb tickled at him an' I tuck him to the bath-room an' fust thing I knowed he grabbed holter me an' shuck me like what you see a cat do a mouse, an' he say ——"

"And he 'd more 'n a million whiskers," interrupted Jimmy, who thought Billy was receiving too much attention, "and he ——"

"One at a time," said the Doctor. "Proceed, William."

"An' he say he 'll bust my brains outer my head if I holler, an' I ain't a-goin' to holler neither, an' he tie me to a chair an' tie my mouth up an' lock the do'——"

"And I comed over," said Jimmy eagerly, "and I run home and I see Mr. Algernon Jones is a robber and I 'phoned to Miss Minerva's beau, and if he 'd brunged what I told him, he would n't never got cracked in the face like Mr. Algernon Jones done crack him, and Billy got to all time let robbers in the house so they can knock mans and little boys down."

"While you stand talking here the scoundrel will get away," said the injured man.

"That is so," agreed Doctor Sanford, "so I'll go and find the Sheriff."

Sarah Jane's huge form loomed up in the back-hall doorway, and she grabbed Jimmy by the arm.

"Yaas," she cried, "you gwine take you a nap is yuh, yuh 'ceitful caterpillar. Come on home dis minute."

"Lemme go, Sarah Jane," protested the little boy, trying to jerk away from her, "I got to stay here and pertec' Billy and Miss Minerva's beau 'cause they 's a robber might come back and tie 'em up and make 'em bleed if I ain't here."

"Did Mr. Algernon Jones make all that blood?" asked an awe-stricken little boy gazing in admiration at the victim of Mr. Jones's energy. "You sho' is a hero to stan' up an' let him knock you down like he done."

"Yes," cried Jimmy, as the black woman dragged him kicking and struggling through the hall, "we 's all heroes, but I bet I 'm the heroest hero they is, and I bet Miss Minerva 's going to be mad 'bout you all spilling all that blood on her nice clean ficor."

"Lemme see yo' big toe what was shot off by all them Yankees and Injuns what you killed in the war," said Billy to Miss Minerva's beau.

The Major smiled at the little boy; a man-to-man smile, full of good comradeship, humor, and understanding. Billy's little heart went out to him at once.

"I can't take off my shoes at present,"

said the veteran. "Well, I must be going; I feel all right now."

Billy looked at him with big, solemn eyes.

"You could n't never go 'thout yo' pants, could you?" he asked, " 'cause Aunt Minerva jest nachelly despises pants."

The man eyed him quizzically.

"Well, no; I don't think I could," he replied; "I don't think I 'd look any better in a Mother Hubbard or a kimono."

The little boy sighed.

"Which you think is the fittenest name," asked he, "Billy or William."

"Billy, Billy," enthusiastically came the reply.

"I like mens," said William Green Hill, "I sho' wisht you could come and live right here with me and Aunt Minerva."

"I wish so, too," said the Major.

CHAPTER XV

BILLY, THE CREDULOUS

FTER the advent and disappearance of the exciting Mr. Jones, Miss Minerva, much to Billy's joy, had a telephone put in the house. He sat in the hall the day it was put in waiting for it to ring.

Jimmy, coming up on the front porch and through the half-open door and seeing him sitting there, rang the door bell just for a joke, ready to burst into a laugh when the other little boy turned around and saw who it was. Billy, however, in his eagerness mistook the ring for the telephone bell and joyfully climbed up on the chair, which he had stationed in readiness. He took down the receiver as he had seen Jimmy do in his home and, without once seeing that little boy standing a few feet from him, he yelled at the top of his lungs:

"Hello! Who is that?"

"This is Marie Yarbrough," replied Jimmy from the doorway, instantly recognizing Billy's mistake.

Marie Yarbrough was a little girl much admired by the two boys, as she had a pony and cart of her very own. However, she lived in a different part of the town and attended another Sunday-School, so they had no speaking acquaintance with her.

"I jus' wanted to talk to you," went on the counterfeit Marie, stifling a laugh and trying to talk like a girl. "I think you 're 'bout the sweetest little boy they is and I want you to come to my party."

"I sho' will," screamed the gratified Billy, "if Aunt Minerva 'll lemme. What make you talk so much like Jimmy?"

"Who? — that little old Jimmy Garner? I hope I don't talk like that chicken, he 's 'bout the measliest boy they is and I like you 'nother sight better 'n him. You 're a plumb jim-dandy, Billy," came from the doorway.

"So 's you," howled back the delighted and flattered Billy.

Jimmy thought he would pop wide open in his efforts to keep from laughing.

"How 'd you like to be my sweetheart?" he asked.

"I 's already promise' to marry Miss Cecilia when I puts on long pants, but if we ever gits a 'vorce I 'd 'nother sight ruther have you 'n anybody.   You can be my lady-frien', anyhow," was the loud reply.

"I 'm coming for you to go riding in my little pony and cart," said a giggling Jimmy.

"All right, I 's going to ask Aunt Minerva to lemme go. Can't we take Jimmy too?"

This was too much for the little boy.   He had held himself in as long as possible.   He burst into a peal of laughter so merry and so loud that Billy, turning, quickly, almost fell out of the chair.

"What you doin', a-listening to me talk to Marie Yarbrough th'oo the telephone?" he questioned angrily.

"Marie your pig's foot," was the inelegant response.   "That was just me a-talking to you all the time.   You all time think you talking to little girls and all time 't ain't nobody but me."

A light dawned upon the innocent one. He promptly hung up the receiver and got down out of the chair.   Before Jimmy was fully aware of his intention, Billy had thrown him to the floor and was giving him a good pommeling.

"Say you got 'nough?" he growled from his position astride of the other boy.

"I got 'nough, Billy," repeated Jimmy.

"Say you sorry you done it."

"I say I sorry I done it," abjectly repeated the younger child. "Get up, Billy, 'fore you bust my stommick open."

"Say you ain't never a-goin' to tell nobody, cross yo' heart," was the next command.

"I say I ain't never going to tell nobody, cross my heart. Get up, Billy, 'fore you make me mad, and ain't no telling what I 'll do to you if I get mad."

"Say you 's a low-down Jezebel skunk."

"I ain't going to say I 'm nothing of the kind," spiritedly replied the under-dog. "You all time wanting somebody to call theirselfs someping. You 're a low-down Isabella skunk yourself."

"You got to say it," insisted the victor, renewing hostilities.

"I 'll say I 'm a Isabella 'cause Isabella discovered America and 's in the Bible," replied the tormented one; "Miss Cecilia 'splained it to me."

Billy accepted his compromise and Jimmy's flattened stomach, relieved of its burden, puffed out to its usual roundness as that little boy rose to his feet, saying:

"Sam Lamb would 'a' died a-laughing, Billy, if he 'd seen you telephoning."

"He 'd better never hear tell of it," was the threatening rejoinder.

CHAPTER XVI

THE HUMBLE PETITION

ILLY, sitting in an old buggy in front of the livery stable, had just engaged in a long and interesting conversation with Sam Lamb. He was getting out of the vehicle when the sharp wire around a broken rod caught in the back of his trousers and tore a great hole. He felt a tingling pain and looked over his shoulder to investigate. Not being satisfied with the result, he turned his back to the negro and anxiously enquired, "Is my breeches tore, Sam?"

"Dey am dat," was the reply, "dey am busted f'm Dan ter Beersheba."

"What I goin' to do 'bout it?" asked the little boy, "Aunt Minerva sho' will be mad. These here 's bran-spankin' new trousers what I ain't never wore tell to-day. Ain't you got a needle an' thread so 's you can fix 'em, Sam?"

"Nary er needle," said Sam Lamb.

"Is my union suit tore, too?" and Billy again turned his back for inspection.

His friend made a close examination.

"Yo' unions is injured plum scanerlous," was his discouraging decision, "and hit 'pears ter me dat yo' hide done suffer too; you's got er turrible scratch."

The child sighed. The injury to the flesh was of small importance, — he could hide that from his aunt — but the rent in his trousers was a serious matter.

"I wish I could git 'em mended 'fore I goes home," he said wistfully.

"I tell you what do," suggested Sam, "I 'low Miss Cecilia 'll holp yeh; jest go by her house an' she 'll darn 'em up fer yuh."

Billy hesitated.

"Well, you see, Sam, me an' Miss Cecilia 's engaged an' we 's fixin' to marry jes' 's soon 's I puts on long pants, an' I 'shame' to ask her. An' I don't berlieve young 'omans patches the breeches of young mans what they's goin' to marry nohow. Do you? Aunt Minerva ain' never patched no breeches for the Major. And then," with a modest blush, "my unions is tore too, an' I ain't got on nothin' else to hide my skin."

Again he turned his back to his friend and, his clouded little face looking over his shoulder, he asked, "Do my meat show, Sam?"

"She am visible ter the naked eye," and Sam Lamb laughed loudly at his own wit.

"I don't believe God pays me much attention nohow," said the little boy dolefully; "ev'y day I gets put to bed 'cause sumpin 's all time a-happenin'. If He 'd had a eye on me like He oughter they would n't a been no snaggin'. Aunt Minerva 's goin' to be mad th'oo an' th'oo."

"May be my ol' 'oman can fix 'em, so 's dey won't be so turrible bad," suggested the negro, " 't aint fer, so you jes' run down ter my cabin an' tell Sukey I say fix dem breeches."

The child needed no second bidding, — he fairly flew. Sam's wife was cooking, but she cheerfully stopped her work to help the little boy. She sewed up his union suit and put a bright blue patch on his brown linen breeches.

Billy felt a little more cheerful, though he still dreaded confessing to his aunt and he loitered along the way till it was nearly dark.

Supper was ready when he got home and he walked into the dining-room with his customary ease and grace. But he took his seat uneasily, and he was so quiet during the meal

and ate so little that his aunt asked him
if he were sick. He was planning in his
mind how to break the news of the day's
disaster to her.

"You are improving, William," she remarked presently, "you have n't got into any
mischief to-day. You have been a mighty
good little boy now for two days."

Billy flushed at the compliment and
shifted uneasily in his seat. That patch
seemed to burn him.

"If God 'd jest do His part," he said darkly, "I would n't never git in no meanness."

After supper Miss Minerva washed the
dishes in the kitchen sink and Billy carried
them back to the dining-room. His aunt
caught him several times prancing sideways
in the most idiotic manner. He was making
a valiant effort to keep from exposing his
rear elevation to her; once he had to walk
backward.

"William," she said sharply, "you will
break my plates. What is the matter with
you to-night?"

A little later they were sitting quietly in
Miss Minerva's room. She was reading
"The Christian at Home," and he was ab-
sently looking at a picture book.

"Sam Lamb's wife Sukey sho' is a beautiful patcher," he remarked, feeling his way.

She made no answering comment, and the discouraged little boy was silent for a few minutes. He had worn Aunt Cindy's many-colored patches too often to be ashamed of this one for himself, but he felt that he would like to draw his aunt out and find how she stood on the subject of patches.

"Aunt Minerva," he presently asked, "what sorter patches 'd you ruther wear on yo' pants, blue patches or brown?"

"On my what?" she asked, looking at him severely over her paper.

"I mean if you 's me," he hastily explained. "Don't you think blue patches is the mos' nat'ral lookin'?"

"What are you driving at, William?" she asked; but without waiting for his answer she went on with her reading.

The child was silent for a long time, his little mind busy, then he began, "Aunt Minerva —— ?"

She peered at him over her glasses a second, then dropped her eyes to the paper where an interesting article on Foreign Missions held her attention.

"Aunt Minerva, I snagged — Aunt Minerva, I snagged my — my skin, to-day."

"Let me see the place," she said absently, her eyes glued to a paragraph describing a cannibal feast.

"I 's a-settin' on it right now," he replied.

Another long silence ensued. Billy resolved to settle the matter.

"I 's gettin' sleepy," he yawned. "Aunt Minerva, I wants to say my prayers and go to bed."

She laid her paper down and he dropped to his knees by her side. He usually sprawled all over her lap during his lengthy devotions, but to-night he clasped his little hands and reared back like a rabbit on its haunches.

After he had rapidly repeated the Lord's prayer, which he had recently learned, and had invoked blessings on all his new friends and never-to-be-forgotten old ones, he concluded with:

"An', O Lord, You done kep' me f'om meddlin' with Aunt Minerva's hose any mo', an' you done kep' me f'om gittin' any mo' Easter eggs, an' playin' any mo' Injun, an' You done kep' me f'om lettin' Mr. Algernon Jones come ag'in, an' now, O

Lord, please don't lemme worry the very
'zistence outer Aunt Minerva any mo' 'n
You can help, like she said I done this
mornin,' an' please, if Thy will be done,
don't lemme tear the next new breeches
what she'll gimme like I done ruint these-
here what I got on."

CHAPTER XVII

A GREEN-EYED BILLY

AVE some candy?" said Miss Cecilia, offering a big box of bonbons to Billy, who was visiting her.

"Where 'd you git 'em?" he asked, as he helped himself generously.

"Maurice sent them to me this morning."

Billy put all his candy back into the box.

"I don't believe I wants noner yo' candy," he said, scowling darkly. "I reckon you likes him better 'n me anyhow, don't you?"

"I love you dearly," she replied.

The child stood in front of her and looked her squarely in the eye. His little form was drawn to its full, proud height, his soft, fair cheeks were flushed, his big, beautiful, grey eyes looked somber and sad.

"Is you in love with that red-headed Maurice Richmond an' jes' a-foolin' o' me?" he asked with dignity.

A bright flush dyed crimson the young lady's pretty face.

She put her arm around the childish, graceful figure and drew the little boy to the sofa beside her.

"Now, honey, you must n't be silly," she said gently, "you are my own, dear, little sweetheart."

"An' I reckon he's yo' own, dear, big sweetheart," said the jealous Billy. "Well, all I got to say is this-here; if he 's a-goin' to come to see you ev'y day then I ain't never comin' no mo'. He 's been a-carryin' on his foolishness 'bout 's long as I can stand it. You got to chose 'tween us right this minute; he come down here mos' ev'y day, he 's tuck you drivin' more'n fifty hunderd times, an' he's give you all the candy you can stuff."

"He is not the only one who comes to see me," she said smiling down at him. "Jimmy comes often and Len Hamner and Will Reid. Don't you want them to come?"

"Don't nobody pay no 'tention to Jimmy," he replied contemptuously; "he ain't nothin' but a baby, an' them other mens can come if you wants 'em to; but," said Billy, with a lover's unerring intuition, "I ain't a-goin' to stand fer that long-legged, sorrel-top Maurice Richmond a-trottin' his great big carkiss down here ev'y minute. I wish Aunt Minerva 'd let me put on long pants to-morrer so 's we could git married." He caught sight of a new ring sparkling on her finger.

"Who give you that ring?" he asked sharply.

"A little bird brought it to me," she said, trying to speak gayly, and blushing again.

"A big, red-headed peckerwood," said Billy savagely.

"Maurice loves you, too,"—she hoped to conciliate him; "he says you are the brightest kid in town."

"Kid," was the scornful echo, "'cause he 's so big and tall, he 's got to call me a kid. Well, he 'd jes' a-wasting' hi'self lovin' me; I don't like him an' I ain't a-goin' to never like him an' soon 's I puts on long pants he 's goin' to get 'bout the worses' lickin' he ever did see.

"Say, does you kiss him like you does me?" he asked presently, looking up at her with serious, unsmiling face.

She hid her embarrassment in a laugh.

"Don't be foolish, Billy," she replied.

"I 'll bet he 's kissed you more 'n fifty hunderd times."

"There 's Jimmy whistling for you," said Miss Cecilia. "How do you two boys make that peculiar whistle? I would recognize it anywhere."

"Is he ever kiss you yet?" asked the child.

"I heard that you and Jimmy whipped Ed Brown because he imitated your own particular whistle. Did you?"

"How many times is he kiss you?" asked Billy.

The young girl put her arm around him and tried to nestle his little body against her own.

"I 'm too big, anyway, for your real sweetheart," she said. "Why, by the time you are large enough to marry I should be an old maid. You must have Frances or Lina for your sweetheart."

"An' let you have Maurice!" he sneered.

She stooped to lay her flushed cheek against his own.

"Honey," she softly said, "Maurice and I are going to be married soon; I love him very much and I want you to love him too."

He pushed her roughly from him.

"An' you jes' 'ceived me all the time," he

cried, "an' me a-lovin' you better 'n anybody
I ever see sence I 's born? An' you a
Sunday-School teacher? I ain't never
a-goin' to trus' nobody no mo'. Good-bye,
Miss Cecilia."

She caught his hand and held it fast; "I
want you and Jimmy to be my little pages
at the wedding, and wear dear little white
satin suits all trimmed with gold braid,"—
she tried to be enthusiastic and arouse his
interest; "and Lina and Frances can be little
flower-girls and we'll have such a beautiful
wedding."

"Jimmy an' Lina an' Frances can be all
the pages an' flower-girls an' brides an'
grooms they wants to, but you can't rope
me in," he scornfully replied. "I 's done
with you an' I ain't never goin' to have me
no mo' sweetheart long 's I live."

CHAPTER XVIII

CLOSER THAN A BROTHER

I T was a bad, rainy day. Jimmy and Billy were playing in Sarah Jane's cabin, she, however, being in happy ignorance of the fact. Her large stays, worn to the preaching the night before, were hanging on the back of a chair.

"Ain't I glad I don' have to wear no corset when I puts on long pants?" remarked Billy, pointing to the article. "Ain't that a big one? It 's twice 's big 's Aunt Minerva's."

"My mama wears a big co'set, too," said Jimmy; "I like fat womans 'nother sight better 'n lean ones. Miss Minerva 's 'bout the skinniest woman they is; when I get married I 'm going to pick me out the fattest wife I can find, so when you set in her lap at night for her to rock you to sleep you 'll have a soft place to put your head, while she sings to you."

"The Major—he 's mos' plump enough for two," said Billy, taking down the stays and trying to hook them around him.

"It sho' is big," he said; "I berlieve it 's big 'nough to go 'round both of us."

"Le's see if 't ain't," was the other boy's ready suggestion.

He stood behind Billy and they put the stays around both little bodies, while, with much squeezing and giggling, Billy hooked them safely up the front. The boys got in front of Sarah Jane's one looking-glass and danced about laughing with glee.

"We 're like the twinses what was growed together like mama read me 'bout," declared the younger child.

Presently they began to feel uncomfortable, especially Jimmy, whose fat, round little middle was tightly compressed.

"Here, unhook this thing, Billy, and le's take her off," he said. "I 'm 'bout to pop open."

"All right," agreed his companion.

He tugged and pulled, but could get only the top and bottom hooks unclasped; the middle ones refused to budge.

"I can't get these-here hooks to come loose," Billy said.

Jimmy put his short, fat arms around him and tried his hand, but with no better success. The stays were such a snug fit that the hooks seemed glued.

"We sho' is in a fix," said Billy gloomily; "look like God all time lettin' us git in trouble."

"You think of more fool stunts to do, William Hill, than any boy they is," cried the other; "you all time want to get us hooked up in Sarah Jane's corset and you all time can't get nobody loose. What you want to get us hooked up in this thing for?"

"You done it yo'self," defended the boy in front with rising passion. "Squeeze in, Jimmy; we jes' boun' to git outer this 'fore somebody finds it out."

He backed the other child close to the wall and pressed so hard against him that Jimmy screamed aloud and began to pound him on the head with his chubby fists.

Billy would not submit tamely to any such treatment. He reached his hand behind him and gave the smaller boy's cheek a merciless pinch. The fight was on. The two little boys, laced up tightly as they were in a stout pair of stays, pinched and scratched, and kicked and jerked. Suddenly

Billy, leaning heavily against Jimmy, threw him flat on his back and fell on top of him.

Bennie Dick, sitting on the floor, had up to this time watched the proceedings with an interested eye; now, thinking murder was being committed, he opened his big, red mouth and emitted a howl that could be heard half a mile. It immediately brought

his mother to the open door. When she saw the children squirming on the floor in her only corset, her indignation knew no bounds.

"You, Jimmy Garner, an' you, too, William Hill, yuh little imps o' Satan, what you doin' in my house? Did n't yo' mammy tell you not to tamper wid me no mo'? Git

up an' come here an' lemme git my co'set
off o' yuh."

Angry as she was she could not keep from
laughing at the sight they presented, as,
with no gentle hand, she unclasped the hooks
and released their imprisoned bodies.

"Billy all time ———— " began Jimmy.

"Billy all time nothin'," said Sarah Jane,
" 't ain't no use fo' to try to lay dis-here
co'set business onto Billy; both o' yuh is
ekally in it. An' me a-aimin' fo' to go to
three fun'els dis week an' a baptizin' on
Sunday. S'pose y' all 'd bruck one o' de
splints, how'd I look a-presidin' at a fun'el
'thout nare co'set on, an' me shape' like
what I is?"

"Who 's dead, Sarah Jane?" asked Jimmy,
hoping to stem the torrent of her wrath.

"Sis' Mary Ellen 's las' husban', Brudder
Littlejohn — dat 's a-who," she replied,
somewhat mollified at his interest.

"When did he die?"— Jimmy pursued his
advantage.

"He got 'way f'om here 'bout moon-down
las' night," she replied, losing sight of her
grievance in his flattering interrogations.
"You know Sis' Littlejohn, she been married
goin' on five times. Dis-here 'll make fo'

gentlemans she done buriet an' dey ain't
nobody can manage a fun'el like she kin;
'pears like hit jes' come natchel to her. She
sho' is done a good part by eb'ry single husban' too, an' she 's figgerin' to outdo all the
yuthers wid Brudder Littlejohn's co'pse."
Sarah Jane almost forgot her little audience
in her intense absorption of her subject.
"She say to me dis mornin', she say, 'Mar-
ri'ge am a lott'ry, Sis Beddinfiel', but I sho'
is drawed some han'some prizes.' She got
'em all laid out side by side in de buryin'
groun' wid er little imige on ebry grabe; an'
Sis Mary Ellen, seein' as she can't read de
writin' on de tombstones, she got a diff'unt
little animal a-settin' on eb'ry head res' so 's
she kin tell which husban' am which. Her
fus' husban' were all time a-huntin', so she
got a little white marble pa'tridge a-restin'
on he' head, an' hit am a mighty console-
ment to a po' widda 'oman fo' to know dat
she can tell de very minute her eyes light
on er grabe which husban' hit am. Her
secon' man he got er mighty kinky, woolly
head an' he mighty meek, so she got a little
white lamb a-settin' on he grabe; an' de nex'
husban' he did n't have nothin' much fo' to
disgueese him f'om de res' 'cep'in' he so

slow an' she might nigh rack her brain off, twell she happen to think 'bout him bein' a Hardshell Baptis' an' so powerful slow, so she jest got a little tarrapim an' sot it on him. Hit sho' am a pretty sight jes' to go in dat buryin' groun' an' look at 'em all, side by side; an' now she got Brudder Little-john to add to de res'. He de onliest one what 's got er patch o' whiskers so she gwine to put a little white cat on he' grabe. Yes, Lord, ef anythink could pearten' a widda 'oman hit would be jes' to know dat yuh could go to de grabeyard any time yuh want to an' look at dat han'some c'llection an' tell 'zactly which am which."

Sarah Jane stopped for breath and Billy hastened to inquire,

"Who else is dead, Sarah Jane?"

" 'T ain't nobody else dead, yit, as I knows on, but my two cousins is turrible low; one 's got a hemrage on de lung an' de yuther 's got a congestin' on de brain, an' I 'lows dey 'll bofe drap off 'twix' now an' sun-up to-morra." Her eyes rolled around and hap-pened to light on her corset. She at once returned to her grievance.

"An' sposin' I had n't 'av' came in here when I did? I'd 'a' had to went to my own

cousins' fun'el 'thout nare co'set.   Y' all
gotta go right to y' all's mamas an' Miss
Minerva dis very minute. I low dey 'll
settle yo' hashes. Don't y' all know dat
Larroes ketch meddlers?"

CHAPTER XIX

TWINS AND A SISSY

MRS. Hamilton and Mrs. Black were sitting on Miss Minerva's veranda talking to her, and Lina and Frances were in the swing with Billy. The attraction proved too great for Jimmy; he impolitely left a disconsolate little visitor sitting on his own porch while he jumped the fence and joined the other children.

"Don't you all wish you could see Mrs. Brown's new twinses?" was his greeting as he took his seat by Billy.

"Where 'd she get 'em?" asked Frances.

"Doctor Sanford tooken 'em to her last night."

"He muster found 'em in a holler stump," remarked Billy. "I knows, 'cause that 's where Doctor Shacklefoot finds aller ol' Aunt Blue-Gum Tempy's Peruny Pearline's, an' me an' Wilkes Booth Lincoln been lookin' in ev'y holler stump we see ever

sence we 's born, an' we ain't never foun' no
baby 't all, 'cause can't nobody but jes'
doctors fin' 'em. I wish he 'd a-give 'em to
Aunt Minerva 'stidder Mrs. Brown."

"I wish he 'd bringed 'em to my mama,"
said Frances.

"I certainly do think he might have given
them to us," declared Lina, "and I 'm going
to tell him so, too. As much money as
father has paid him for doctor's bills and as
much old, mean medicine as I have taken
just to 'commodate him; then he gives
babies to everybody but us."

"I 'm awful glad he never give 'em to my
mama," said Jimmy, " 'cause I never could
had no more fun; they 'd be stuck right
under my nose all time, and all time put
their mouth in everything you want to do,
and all time meddling. You can't fool me
'bout twinses. But I wish I could see 'em!
They so weakly they got to be hatched in a
nincubator."

"What 's that?" questioned Frances.

"That 's a someping what you hatches
chickens and babies in when they 's delicate,
and ain't got 'nough breath and ain't got
they eyes open and ain't got no feathers on,"
explained Jimmy.

"Reckon we can see 'em?" she asked.

"See nothing!" sniffed the little boy. "Ever since Billy let Mr. Algernon Jones whack Miss Minerva's beau we can't do nothing at all 'thout grown folks 'r' stuck right under your nose. I 'm jes' cramped to death."

"When I 'm a mama," mused Frances, "I hope Doctor Sanford 'll bring me three little twinses, and two Maltese kittens, and a little Japanee, and a monkey, and a parrit."

"When I 'm a papa," said Jimmy, "I don' want no babies at all, all they 's good for is jus' to set 'round and yell."

"Look like God 'd sho' be busy a-makin' so many babies," remarked Billy.

"Why, God don' have none 'a the trouble," explained Jimmy. "He 's just got Him a baby factory in Heaven like the chair factory and the canning factory down by the railroad, and angels jus' all time make they arms and legs, like niggers do at the chair factory, and all God got to do is jus' glue 'em together, and stick in their souls. God 's got 'bout the easiest job they is."

"I thought angels jes' clam' the golden stair and play they harps," said Billy.

"Ain't we going to look sweet at Miss

Cecilia's wedding," said Frances, after a short silence.

"I 'll betcher I 'll be the cutest kid in that church," boasted Jimmy conceitedly. "You coming, ain't you, Billy?"

"I gotter go," answered that jilted swain, gloomily, "Aunt Minerva ain't got nobody to leave me with at home. I jes' wish she 'd git married."

"Why would n't you be a page, Billy?" asked Lina.

" 'Cause I did n't hafto," was the snappish reply.

"I bet my mama give her the finest present they is," bragged the smaller boy; "I reckon it cost 'bout a million dollars."

"Mother gave her a handsome cut-glass vase," said Lina.

"It looks like Doctor Sanford would 've give Miss Cecilia those twinses for a wedding present," said Frances.

"Who is that little boy sitting on your porch, Jimmy?" asked Lina, noticing for the first time a lonely-looking child.

"That's Leon Tipton, Aunt Ella's little boy. He just come out from Memphis to spend the day with me and I 'll be awful glad when he goes home; he's 'bout the

stuck-up-est kid they is, and skeery? He 's
'bout the 'fraidest young un ever you see.
And look at him now? Wears long curls
like a girl and don't want to never get his
clean clo'es dirty."

"I think he 's a beautiful little boy,"
championed Lina. "Call him over here,
Jimmy."

"Naw, I don't want to. You all 'll like
him a heap better over there; he 's one o'
these-here kids what the furder you get
'way from 'em, the better you like 'em."

"He sho' do look lonesome," said Billy;
" 'vite him over, Jimmy."

"Leon!" screamed his cousin, "you can
come over here if you wantta."

The lonesome-looking little boy promptly
accepted the invitation, and came primly
through the two gates. He walked proudly
to the swing and stood, cap in hand, waiting
for an introduction.

"Why did n't you clam' the fence, 'stead
of coming th'oo the gates?" growled Jimmy.
"You 'bout the prissiest boy they is. Well,
why don't you set down?"

"Introduce me, please," said the elegant
little city boy.

"Interduce your grandma's pussy cats," mocked Jimmy. "Set down, I tell you."

Frances and Lina made room for him between them and soon gave him their undivided attention, to the intense envy and disgust of the other two little boys.

"I am Lina Hamilton," said the little girl on his right.

"And I 'm Frances Black, and Jimmy ought to be 'shamed to treat you like he does."

"I knows a turrible skeery tale," remarked a malicious Billy, looking at Lina and Frances. "If y' all wa'n't girls I 'd tell it to you."

"We are n't any more scared 'n you, William Hill," cried Frances, her interest at once aroused; "I already know 'bout 'raw meat and bloody bones' and nothing 's scarier 'n that."

"And I know 'Fe, Fi, Fo, Fum, I smell the blood of an Englishman. Be he alive or be he dead, I'll ground his bones to make me bread,'" said Lina.

"This-here tale," continued Billy, glueing his big eyes to those of the little stranger, "is one Tabernicle learnt fer a speech at school. It 's all 'bout a 'oman what was

buriet in a graveyard with a diamant ring
on her finger, an' a robber come in the
night———" The child's tones were gut-
tural, thrilling, and hair-raising as he glared
into the eyes of the effeminate Leon, "an'
a robber come in the night an' try to cut it
off, an' ha'nts was groanin' an' the win' moan
'oo-oo' an'———"

Leon could stand it no longer.

"I am going right back," he cried rising
with round, frightened eyes, "I am not going
to sit here and listen to you, scaring little
girls to death. You are a bad boy to scare
Lina and Frances and I am not going to
associate with you;" and this champion of
the fair sex stalked with dignity across the
yard to the gate.

"I 'm no more scared 'n nothing," and
indignant Frances hurled at his back. "You
're just scared yourself."

Jimmy giggled happily. "What 'd I tell
you all," he cried, gleefully. "Lina and
Frances got to all time set little 'fraid cats
'tween 'em," he snorted. "It 's just like I
tell you, he 's the sissyest boy they is; and
he don't care who kiss him neither; he 'll let
any woman kiss him what wants to. Can't
no woman at all 'cepting my mama and Miss

Cecilia kiss me. But Leon is 'bout the kissingest kid they is; why, he'd just as soon 's not let Frances and Lina kiss him; he ain't got no better sense. 'Course I gotta let Miss Cecilia kiss me 'cause she's 'bout the plumpest Sunday-School teacher they is and the Bible say 'If your Sunday-School teacher kiss you on one cheek turn the other cheek and let her kiss you on that, too,' and I all time bound to do what the Bible say. You 'd better call him back, Frances, and kiss him, you and Lina 're so stuck on him."

"I would n't kiss him to save his life," declared Frances; "he 's got the spindliest legs I ever saw."

CHAPTER XX

RISING IN THE WORLD

THE painter had just finished putting a bright green coat of paint upon the low, flat roof of Miss Minerva's long back-porch. And he left his ladder leaning against the house while he went inside to confer with her in regard to some other work.

Billy, Jimmy, Frances, and Lina had been playing "Fox and Geese." Running around the house they spied the ladder and saw no owner to deny them.

'Le 's clam' up and get on top the porch," suggested Jimmy.

"Aunt Minerva 'll put me to bed if I do," said Billy.

"Mother 'll make me learn a whole page of the catechism if I climb a ladder," said Lina.

"My mama 'll shut me up in the closet, but our mamas are n't bound to know 'bout it,"

—this from Frances. "Come on, let 's climb up."

"I ain't never promise not to clam' no ladder but ———" Billy hesitated.

"You-all 'bout the skeeriest folks they is," sneered Jimmy. "Mama 'll whip me going and coming if she finds out 'bout it, but I ain't skeered. I dare anybody to dare me to clam' up."

"I dare you to climb this ladder," responded an accommodating Frances.

"I ain't never tooken a dare yet," boasted the little boy proudly, his foot on the bottom rung. "Who 's going to foller me?"

"Don't we have fun?" cried a jubilant Frances.

"Yes," answered Jimmy; "if grown folks don't all time be watching you and sticking theirselfs in your way."

"If people would let us alone," remarked Lina, "we could enjoy ourselves every day."

"But grown folks got to be so pertic'lar with you all time," cried Jimmy, "they don't never want us to play together."

He led the way up the ladder, followed by Frances and Billy; and Lina brought up the rear. The children ran the long length of the porch leaving their footprints on the fresh, sticky paint.

"Will it wash off?" asked Frances, looking gloomily down at her feet, which seemed to be encased in green moccasins.

At that moment she slipped and fell sprawling on top of the roof. When the others helped her to her feet, she was a sight to behold, her white dress splotched with vivid green from top to bottom.

"If that ain't jus' like you, Frances," Jimmy exclaimed; "you all time got to fall down and get paint on your dress so we can't 'ceive nobody. Now our mamas bound to know 'bout us clamming up here."

"They would know it anyhow," mourned Lina; "we'll never get this paint off of our feet. We had better get right down and see if we can't wash some of it off."

While they were talking the owner of the ladder, who had not noticed them—and was deaf in the bargain—had quietly removed it from the back-porch and carried it around to the front of the house.

The children looked at each other in consternation when they perceived their loss.

"What we goin' to do now?" asked Billy.

"If this ain't just like Billy, all time got to

perpose to clam' a ladder and all time got
to let the ladder get loose from him,"
growled Jimmy. "We done cooked a goose
egg, this time. You got us up here, Billy,
how you going to get us down?"

"I did n't, neither."

"Well, it 's Miss Minerva's house and
she 's your aunt and we 's your company
and you got to be 'sponsible."

"I can clam' down this-here post," said
the responsible party.

"I can climb down it, too," seconded
Frances.

"You can't clam' down nothing at all,"
said Jimmy contemptuously. "Talk 'bout
you can clam' down a post; you 'd fall and
bust yourself wide open; you 'bout the clum-
siest girl there is; 'sides, your legs 're too
fat."

"We can holla," was Lina's suggestion.

"And have grown folks laughing fit to pop
their sides open? I 'm 'shame' to go any-
wheres now 'cause folks all time telling me
when I 'm going to dye some more Easter
eggs! Naw, we better not holler," said
Jimmy. "Ain't you going to do nothing.
Billy?"

"I 'll jest slide down this-here post and git

the painter man to bring his ladder back. Y' all wait up here."

Billy's solution of the difficulty seemed the safest, and they were soon released from their elevated prison.

"I might as well go home and be learning the catechism," groaned Lina.

"I 'm going to get right in the closet soon 's I get to my house," said Frances.

"Go on and put on your night-shirt, Billy."

Billy took himself to the bath-room and scrubbed and scrubbed; but the paint refused to come off. He tiptoed by the kitchen where his aunt was cooking dinner and ran into his own room.

He found the shoes and stockings which were reserved for Sunday wear, and soon had them upon his little feet.

Miss Minerva rang the dinner-bell and he walked quietly into the dining-room trying to make as little noise and to attract as little attention from his aunt as possible; but she fastened her eyes at once upon his feet.

"What are you doing with your shoes on, William?" she asked.

Billy glanced nonchalantly at her.

"Don't you think, Aunt Minerva," he made answer, "I 's gittin' too big to go 'thout any shoes? I 's mos' ready to put on long pants, an' how 'd I look, I 'd jest like to know, goin' roun' barefooted an' got on long breeches. I don' believe I 'll go barefooted no mo'—I'll jest wear my shoes ev'y day."

"I just believe you won't. Go take them off at once and hurry back to your dinner."

"Lemme jest wait tell I eats," he begged, hoping to postpone the evil hour of exposure.

"No, go at once, and be sure and wash your hands."

Miss Minerva spied the paint the instant he made his second entrance and immediately inquired, "How did you get that paint on your feet?"

The little boy took his seat at the table and looked up at her with his sweet, attractive, winning smile.

"Paint pertec's little boys' feets," he said, "an' keeps 'em f'om gittin' hurted, Aunt Minerva, don't it?"

Miss Minerva laid down her fork and gave her nephew her undivided attention.

"You have been getting into mischief again, I see, William; now tell me all about it. Are you afraid of me?"

"Yas 'm," was his prompt response, "an' I don't want to be put to bed neither. The Major he would n't put little boys to bed day times."

She blushed and eyed him thoughtfully. She was making slow progress with the child, she knew, yet she still felt it her stern duty to be very strict with him and, having laid down certain rules to rear him by, she wished to adhere to them.

"William," she said after he had made a

full confession, "I won't punish you this time for I know that Jimmy led you into it but ———."

"Naw 'm, Jimmy did n't. Me an' him an' Frances an' Lina's all 'sponsible, but I promise you, Aunt Minerva, not to clam' no mo' ladders."

CHAPTER XXI

PRETENDING REALITY

THE chain-gang had been working in the street not far from Miss Minerva's house, and Lina, Frances, Billy and Jimmy had hung on her front fence for an hour, watching them with eager interest. The negroes were chained together in pairs, and guarded by two, big, burly white men.

"Let's us play chain-gang," suggested Jimmy.

"Where we goin' to git a chain?" queried Billy; "'t won't be no fun 'thout a lock an' chain."

"I can get the lock and chain off 'm Sarah Jane's cabin."

"Yo' mama don't 'low you to go to her cabin," said Billy.

"My mama don't care if I just borra a lock and chain; so I'm going to get it."

"I'm going to be the perlice of the gang," said Frances.

"Perlice nothing. You all time talking 'bout you going to be the perlice," scoffed Jimmy. "I 'm going to be the perlice myself."

"No, you are not," interposed Lina, firmly. "Billy and I are the tallest and we are going to be the guards, and you and Frances must be the prisoners."

"Well, I ain't going to play 'thout I can be the boss of the niggers. It 's Sarah Jane's chain and she 's my mama's cook, and I 'm going to be what I please."

"I 'll tell you what do," was Billy's suggestion, "we'll take it turn about; me an' Lina 'll firs' be the perlice an' y' all be the chain-gang, an' then we 'll be the niggers an' y' all be the bosses."

This arrangement was satisfactory, so the younger boy climbed the fence and soon returned with a short chain and padlock.

Billy chained Jimmy and Frances together by two round, fat ankles and put the key to the lock in his pocket.

"We must decide what crimes they have committed," said Lina.

"Frances done got 'rested fer shootin' craps an' Jimmy done got 'rested fer 'sturbin' public worship," said the other boss.

"Naw, I ain't neither," objected the male member of the chain-gang, "I done cut my woman with a razor 'cause I see her racking down the street like a proud coon with another gent, like what Sarah Jane's brother told me he done at the picnic."

The children played happily together for half an hour, Billy and Lina commanding, and the prisoners, entering thoroughly into the spirit of the game, according prompt obedience to their bosses. At last the captives wearied of their rôle and clamored for an exchange of parts.

"All right," agreed Lina. "Get the key, Billy, and we 'll be the chain-gang."

Billy put his right hand in his pocket but found no key there; he tried the other pocket with the same success; he felt in his blouse, he looked in his cap, he jumped up and down, he nearly shook himself to pieces all without avail; the key had disappeared as if by magic.

"I berlieve y' all done los' that key," concluded he.

"Maybe it dropped on the ground," said Frances.

They searched the yard over, but the key was not to be found.

"Well, if that ain't just like you, Billy," cried Jimmy, "you all time perposing to play chain-gang and you all time lose the key."

Lina grew indignant.

"You proposed this yourself, Jimmy Garner," she said; "we never would have thought of playing chain-gang but for you."

"It looks like we can't never do anything at all," moaned Frances, "'thout grown folks 've got to know 'bout it."

"Yes, and laugh fit to pop theirselfs open," said her fellow-prisoner. "I can't never pass by Owen Gibbs and Len Hamner now 'thout they laugh just like idjets and grin just like pole-cats."

"I ain't never hear tell of a pole-cat grin-nin'," corrected Billy, "he jes' smell worser 'n what a billy goat do."

"It is Chessy cats that grin," explained Lina.

"Look like folks would get 'em a lot of pole-cats stead o' chillens always hafto be wearing assfetty bags 'round their nakes, so 's they can keep off whopping-cough," said Frances.

"You can't wear a pole-cat roun' yo' nake," grinned Billy.

"And Len Hamner all time now asking me," Jimmy continued, "when I'm going to wear Sarah Jane's co'set to Sunday-School. Grown folks 'bout the lunatickest things

they is. Ain't you going to unlock this chain, Billy?" he demanded.

"What I got to unlock it with?" asked Billy.

As Jimmy's father was taking the crest-fallen chain-gang to the blacksmith shop to have their fetters removed, they had to pass by the livery stable; and Sam Lamb, bent double with intoxicating mirth at their predicament, yelled:

"Lordee! Lordee! Y' all sho' is de out-landishest kids 'twixt de Bad Place an' de moon."

CHAPTER XXII

A TRANSACTION IN MUMPS

ON'T you come near me," screamed Billy, sauntering slowly and deliberately toward the dividing fence; "keep way f'om me; they 's ketchin'."

Jimmy was sitting on his front steps and the proverbial red flag could not have excited a bull to quicker action. He hopped down the steps and ran across his own yard toward Billy as fast as his short, fat legs could carry him.

"Git 'way f'om me; you 'll ketch 'em if you teches me," warned Billy; "an' you too little to have 'em," and he waved an authoritative hand at the other child. But Jimmy's curiosity was aroused to the highest pitch. He promptly jumped the fence and gazed at his chum with critical admiration.

"What 's the matter," he inquired, "you got the toothache?"

"Toothache!" was the scornful echo,

"well, I reckon not. Git back; don't you
tech 'em; you ain't ol' 'nough to have 'em."

Billy's head was swathed in a huge, white
cloth; his usually lean little cheeks were
puffed out till he resembled a young hippo-
potamus, and his pretty grey eyes were
almost invisible.

"You better git 'way f'om me an' don't
tech 'em, like I tells you," he reiterated.
"Aunt Minerva say you ain't never had 'em
an' she say fer me to make you keep 'way
f'om me 'cause you ain't a ol' chile like what
I is."

"You ain't but six," retorted angry Jimmy,
"and I 'll be six next month; you all time
trying to 'suade little boys to think you 're
'bout a million years old. What 's the
matter with you, anyhow? You 'bout the
funniest looking kid they is."

Billy theatrically touched a distended
cheek. "These here is mumps," he said
impressively; "an' when you got 'em you
can make grown folks do perzactly what
you want 'em to. Aunt Minerva 's in the
kitchen right now makin' me a 'lasses custard if I'll be good an' stay right in the
house an' don't come out here in the yard
an' don't give you the mumps. Course I

can't tech that custard now 'cause I done come out here an' it ain't honer'ble; but she 's makin' it jes' the same. You better git 'way f'om me an' not tech 'em; you too little to have 'em."

"Are they easy to ketch?" asked the other little boy eagerly; "lemme jest tech 'em one time, Billy."

"Git 'way, I tell you," warned the latter with a superior air. To increase Jimmy's envy he continued: "Grown folks tries to see how nice they can be to chillens what 's got the mumps. Aunt Minerva ain't been impedent to me to-day; she lemme do jest 'bout like I please; it sho' is one time you can make grown folks step lively." He looked at Jimmy meditatively, "It sho' is a plumb pity you ain't a ol' chile like what I is an' can't have the mumps. Yo' ma 'd be skeered to spank you, skeered she 'd injuh yo' mumps. Don't you come any closter to me," he again warned, "you too little to have 'em."

"I 'll give you five peewees if you 'll lemme tech 'em so 's I can get 'em," pleaded the younger boy.

Billy hesitated. "You mighty little ——" he began.

"And my stoney," said the other child eagerly.

"If you was a ol' little boy," said Billy, "it would n't make no diffunce; I don't want to make yo' ma mad an' Aunt Minerva say for me to keep 'way f'om you anyhow, though I did n't make her no promises."

Jimmy grew angry.

'You 're the stingiest Peter they is, William Hill," he cried; "won't let nobody tech your old mumps. My cousin in Memphis 's got the measles; you just wait till I get 'em."

Billy eyed him critically.

"If you was ol'——" he was beginning.

Jimmy thought he saw signs of his yielding.

"And I'll give you my china egg, too," he quickly proposed.

"Well, jest one tech," agreed Billy; "an' I ain't a-goin' to be 'sponsible neither," and he poked out a swollen jaw for Jimmy to touch.

Ikey Rosenstein at this moment was spied by the two little boys as he was walking jauntily by the gate.

"You better keep 'way f'om here, Goose-Grease," Jimmy yelled at him; "you better

get on the other side the street. Billy here
's got the mumps an' he lemme tech 'em
so 's I can get 'em, so 's my papa and mama
'll lemme do just perzactly like I want to;
but you 're a Jew and Jews ain't got no
business to have the mumps, so you better
get 'way. I paid Billy 'bout a million
dollars' worth to lemme tech his mumps,"
he said proudly. "Get 'way; you can't have
'em."

Ikey had promptly stopped at the gate.

"What 'll you take, Billy, to lemme get
'em?" he asked, his commercial spirit at once
aroused.

"What 'll you gimme?" asked he of the
salable commodity, with an eye to a
bargain.

Ikey pulled out a piece of twine and a
blue glass bead from his pocket and offered
them to the child with the mumps. These
received a contemptuous rejection.

"You can do perzactly like you please
when you got the mumps," insinuated
Jimmy, who had seemingly allied himself
with Billy as a partner in business; "grown
folks bound to do what little boys want 'em
to when you got the mumps."

Ikey increased his bid by the stub of a

lead pencil, but it was not until he had
parted with his most cherished pocket pos-
sessions that he was at last allowed to place
a gentle finger on the protuberant cheek.

Two little girls with their baby-buggies
were seen approaching.

"G' 'way from here, Frances, you and
Lina," howled Jimmy. "Don't you come in

here; me and Billy 's got the mumps and
you-all 'r' little girls and ought n' to have
'em. Don't you come near us; they 're
ketching."

The two little girls immediately opened

the gate, crossed the yard, and stood in front
of Billy. They inspected him with admiration; he bore their critical survey with
affected unconcern and indifference, as be-
fitted one who had attained such prominence.

"Don't tech 'em," he commanded, waving
them off as he leaned gracefully against the
fence.

"I teched 'em," boasted the younger boy.
"What 'll you all give us if we 'll let you
put your finger on 'em?"

"I ain't a-goin' to charge little girls nothin'," said the gallant Billy, as he proffered
his swollen jowl to each in turn.

A little darkey riding a big black horse
was galloping by; Jimmy hailed and halted
him.

"You better go fast," he shrieked. "Me
and Billy and Frances and Lina 's got the
mumps and you ain't got no business to
have 'em 'cause you 're a nigger, and you
better take your horse to the lib'ry stable
'cause he might ketch 'em too."

The negro boy dismounted and hitched
his horse to the fence. "I gotter little
tarrapim —" he began insinuatingly.

And thus it came to pass that there was
an epidemic of mumps in the little town of

Covington, and William Green Hill grew rich in marbles, in tops, in strings, in toads, in chewing gum, and in many other things which comprise the pocket treasures of little boys.

CHAPTER XXIII

THE INFANT MIND SHOOTS

ISS MINERVA had bought a book for Billy entitled "Stories of Great and Good Men," which she frequently read to him for his education and improvement. These stories related the principal events in the lives of the heroes but never mentioned any names, always asking at the end, "Can you tell me who this man was?"

Her nephew heard the stories so often that he had some expression or incident by which he could identify each, without paying much attention while she was reading.

He and his aunt had just settled themselves on the porch for a reading.

Jimmy was on his own porch cutting up funny capers, and making faces for the other child's amusement.

"Lemme go over to Jimmy's, Aunt Minerva," pleaded her nephew, "an' you can

read to me to-night. I 'd a heap ruther not
hear you read right now. It 'll make my
belly ache."

Miss Minerva looked at him severely.

"William," she enjoined, "don't you want
to be a smart man when you grow up?"

"Yes 'm," he replied, without much en-
thusiasm. "Well, jes' lemme ask Jimmy to
come over here an' set on the other sider
you whils' you read. He ain't never hear
'bout them tales, an' I s'pec' he 'd like to
come."

"Very well," replied his flattered and
gratified relative, "call him over."

Billy went to the fence, where he sig-
naled Jimmy to meet him.

"Aunt Minerva say you come over an'
listen to her read some er the pretties' tales
you ever hear," he said, as if conferring a
great favor.

"Naw, sirree-bob!" was the impolite response across the fence, "them 'bout the
measliest tales they is. I 'll come if she 'll
read my Uncle Remus book."

"Please come on," begged Billy, dropping
the patronizing manner that he had assumed,
in hope of inducing his chum to share his
martyrdom. "You know Aunt Minerva 'd

die in her tracks 'fore she 'd read Uncle
Remus. You 'll like these-here tales 'nother
sight better anyway. I 'll give you my
stoney if you'll come."

"Naw; you ain't going to get me in no
such box as that. If she 'd just read seven
or eight hours I would n't mind; but she 'll
get you where she wants you and read 'bout
a million hours. I know Miss Minerva."

Billy's aunt was growing impatient.

"Come, William," she called. "I am waiting for you."

Jimmy went back to his own porch and
the other boy joined his kinswoman.

"Why would n't Jimmy come?" she asked.

"He — he ain't feeling very well," was the
considerate rejoinder.

"Once there was a little boy who was
born in Virginia ———" began Miss Minerva.

"Born in a manger," repeated the inat-
tentive little boy to himself, "I knows who
that was." So, this important question settled in his mind, he gave himself up to the
full enjoyment of his chum and to the giving
and receiving secret signals, the pleasure of
which was decidedly enhanced by the fear
of imminent detection.

"Father, I can not tell a lie, I did it

with my little hatchet,——" read the thin, monotonous voice at his elbow.

Billy laughed aloud — at that minute Jimmy was standing on his head waving two chubby feet in the air.

"William," said his aunt reprovingly, peering at him over her spectacles, "I don't see anything to laugh at,"— and she did not, but then she was in ignorance of the little conspiracy.

"He was a good and dutiful son and he studied his lessons so well that when he was only seventeen years old he was employed to survey vast tracts of land in Virginia ——"

Miss Minerva emphasized every word, hoping thus to impress her nephew. But he was so busy, keeping one eye on her and one on the little boy on the other porch, that he did not have time to use his ears at all and so did not hear one word.

"Leaving his camp fires burning to deceive the enemy, he stole around by a circuitous route, fell upon the British and captured ——"

Billy held up his hands to catch a ball which Jimmy made believe to throw.

Miss Minerva still read on, unconscious of her nephew's inattention:

"The suffering at Valley Forge had been intense during the winter ——"

Billy made a pretense behind his aunt's upright back of throwing a ball while the other child held up two fat little hands to receive it.   Again he laughed aloud as Jimmy spat on his hands and ground the imaginary ball into his hip.

She looked at him sternly over her glasses:

"What makes you so silly?" she inquired, and without waiting for a reply went on with her reading; she was nearing the close now and she read carefully and deliberately.

"And he was chosen the first president of the United States ——."

Billy put his hands to his ears and wriggled his fingers at Jimmy, who promptly returned the compliment.

"He had no children of his own, so he is called the Father of his Country."

Miss Minerva closed the book, turned to the little boy at her side, and asked:

"Who was this great and good man, William?"

"Jesus," was his ready answer, in an appropriately solemn little voice.

"Why, William Green Hill!" she exclaimed in disgust. "What are you thinking of? I don't believe you heard one word that I read."

Billy was puzzled; he was sure she had said "Born in a manger." "I didn't hear her say nothin' 'bout bulrushes," he thought, "so 't ain't Moses; she did n't say 'log cabin,' so 't ain't Ab'aham Lincoln; she did n't say 'Thirty cents look down upon you,' so 't ain't Napolyon. I sho' wish I 'd paid 'tention."

"Jesus!" his aunt was saying, "born in Virginia and first president of the United States!"

"George Washin'ton, I aimed to say," triumphantly screamed the little boy, who had received his cue.

CHAPTER XXIV

A FLAW IN THE TITLE

OME on over," invited Jimmy.

"All right; I believe I will," responded Billy, running to the fence. His aunt's peremptory voice arrested his footsteps.

"William, come here!" she called from the porch.

He reluctantly retraced his steps.

"I am going back to the kitchen to bake a cake and I want you to promise me not to leave the yard."

"Lemme jes' go over to Jimmy's a little while," he begged.

"No; you and Jimmy can not be trusted together; you are sure to get into mischief, and his mother and I have decided to keep the fence between you for a while. Now, promise me that you will stay right in my yard."

Billy sullenly gave her the promise and she went back to her baking.

"That 's always the way now," he said, meeting his little neighbor at the fence, "ever sence Aunt Minerva got onto this-here promisin' business, I don' have no freedom 't all. It 's 'William, promise me this,' an' it 's 'William, don't ferget yo' promise now,' tell I 's jes' plumb sick 'n tired of it. She know I ain't goin' back on my word an' she jest nachelly gits the 'vantage of me; she 'bout the hardest 'oman to manage I ever seen sence I 's born."

"I can nearly all time make my mama do anything 'most if I jus' keep on trying and keep on a-begging," bragged the other boy; "I just say 'May I, mama?' and she 'll all time say, 'No, go 'way from me and lemme 'lone,' and I just keep on, 'May I, mama? May I, mama? May I, mama?' and toreckly she 'll say, 'Yes, go on and lemme read in peace.' "

"Aunt Minerva won't give in much," said Billy. "When she say 'No, William,' 't ain't no use 't all to beg her; you jest wastin' yo' breath. When she put her foot down it got to go just like she say; she sho' do like to have her own way better 'n any 'oman I ever see."

"She 'bout the mannishest woman they is," agreed Jimmy. "She got you under her thumb, Billy. I don' see what womans 're made fo' if you can't beg 'em into things. I would n't let no old spunky Miss Minerva get the best of me that 'way. Come on, anyhow."

"Naw, I can't come," was the gloomy reply; "if she 'd jest tol' me not to, I coulder went but she made me promise, an' I ain't never goin' back on my word. You come over to see me."

"I can't," came the answer across the fence; "I 'm earning me a baseball mask. I done already earnt me a mitt. My mama don't never make me promise her nothing, she just pays me to be good. That 's huc-come I 'm 'bout to get 'ligion and go to the mourner's bench. She 's gone up town now and if I don't go outside the yard while she 's gone, she 's going to gimme a baseball mask. You got a ball what you bringed from the plantation, and I 'll have a bat and mitt and mask and we can play ball some. Come on over just a little while; you ain't earning you nothing like what I 'm doing."

"Naw; I promis' her not to an' I ain't ever goin' to break my promise."

"Well, then, Mr. Promiser," said Jimmy, "go get your ball and we'll th'ow 'cross the fence. I can't find mine."

Billy kept his few toys and playthings in a closet, which was full of old plunder. As he reached for his ball something fell at his feet from a shelf above. He picked it up, and ran excitedly into the yard.

"Look, Jimmy," he yelled, "here 's a baseball mask I found in the closet."

Jimmy, forgetful of the fact that he was to be paid for staying at home, immediately rolled over the fence and ran eagerly toward his friend. They examined the article in question with great care.

"It looks perzactly like a mask," announced Jimmy after a thorough inspection, "and yet it don't." He tried it on. "It don't seem to fit your face right," he said.

Sarah Jane was bearing down upon them. "Come back home dis minute, Jimmy!" she shrieked, "want to ketch some mo' contagwous 'seases, don't yuh? What dat y' all got now?" As she drew nearer a smile of recognition and appreciation overspread her big good-natured face. Then she burst into a loud, derisive laugh. "What y' all gwine to do wid Miss Minerva's old bustle?" she enquired. "Y' all sho' am de contaritest chillens in dis here copperation."

"Bustle?" echoed Billy, "What 's a bustle?"

"Dat-ar 's a bustle — dat 's what 's a bustle. Ladies useto wear 'em 'cause dey so stylish to make they dresses stick out in the back. Come on home, Jimmy, 'fore yuh ketch de yaller jandis er de epizootics; yo' ma tol' yuh to stay right at home."

"Well, I 'm coming, ain't I?" scowled the little boy. "Mama need n't to know nothing 'thout you tell."

"Would you take yo' mama's present now, Jimmy?" asked Billy; "you ain't earnt it."

"Would n't you?" asked Jimmy, doubt-fully.

"Naw, I would n't, not 'thout I tol' her."

"Well, I 'll tell her I just comed over a minute to see 'bout Miss Minerva's bustle," he agreed as he again tumbled over the fence.

A little negro boy, followed by a tiny, white dog, was passing by Miss Minerva's gate.

Billy promptly flew to the gate and hailed

him. Jimmy, looking around to see that
Sarah Jane had gone back to the kitchen, as
promptly rolled over the fence and joined
him.

"Lemme see yo' dog," said the former.

"Ain't he cute?" said the latter.

The little darkey picked up the dog and
passed it across the gate.

"I wish he was mine," said the smaller
child, as he took the soft, fluffy little ball
in his arms; "what 'll you take for him?"

The negro boy had never seen the dog
before, but he immediately accepted the
ownership thrust upon him and answered
without hesitation, "I'll take a dollar for
her."

"I ain't got but a nickel. Billy, ain't you
got 'nough money to put with my nickel to
make a dollar?

"Naw; I ain't
got a red cent."

"I 'll tell you
what we 'll do,"
suggested Jim-
my; "we 'll
t r a d e you a
baseball mask
for him. My

mama 's going to gimme a new mask 'cause
I all time stay at home, so we 'll trade you
our old one. Go get it, Billy."

Thus commanded Billy ran and picked up
the bustle where it lay neglected on the
grass, and handed it to the quasi-owner of
the puppy. The deal was promptly closed
and a black little negro went grinning down
the street with Miss Minerva's ancient bustle
tied across his face, leaving behind him a
curly-haired dog.

"Ain't he sweet?" said Jimmy, hugging
the fluffy white ball close to his breast, "we
got to name him, Billy."

"Le's name her Peruny Pearline," was
the suggestion of the other joint owner.

"He ain't going to be name' nothing at all
like that," declared Jimmy; "you all time got
to name our dogs the scalawaggest name
they is. He 's going to be name' 'Sam
Lamb' 'cause he 's my partner."

"She 's a girl dog," argued Billy, "an' she
can't be name' no man's name. If she could
I 'd call her Major."

"I don't care what sort o' dog he is, girl
or boy, he 's going to be name' 'Sam Lamb.'
Pretty Sam! Pretty Sam!" and he fondly
stroked the little animal's soft head.

"Here, Peruny! Here, Peruny!" and Billy
tried to snatch her away.

The boys heard a whistle; the dog heard
it, too. Springing from the little boy's arms
Sam Lamb Peruny Pearline ran under the
gate and flew to meet her master, who was
looking for her.

CHAPTER XXV

EDUCATION AND ITS PERILS

I T was a warm day in early August and the four children were sitting contentedly in the swing. They met almost every afternoon now, but were generally kept under strict surveillance by Miss Minerva.

" 'T won't be long 'fore we 'll all hafto go to school," remarked Frances, "and I 'll be mighty sorry; I wish we did n't ever hafto go to any old school."

"I wisht we knowed how to read an' write when we 's born," said Billy. "If I was God I 'd make all my babies so 's they is already eddicated when they gits born. Reckon if we 'd pray ev'y night an' ask God, He 'd learn them babies what He 's makin' on now how to read an' write?"

"I don' care nothing at all 'bout them babies," put in Jimmy, " 't ain't going to do us no good if all the new babies what Docto,

Sanford finds can read and write; it 'd jes'
make 'em the sassiest things ever was.
'Sides, I got plenty things to ask God for
'thout fooling long other folks' brats, and I
ain't going to meddle with God's business
nohow."

"Did you all hear what Miss Larrimore,
who teaches the little children at school,
said about us?" asked Lina importantly.

"Naw," they chorused, "what was it?"

"She told the Super'ntendent," was the
reply of Lina, pleased with herself and with
that big word, "that she would have to have
more money next year, for she heard that
Lina Hamilton, Frances Black, William
Hill, and Jimmy Garner were all coming to
school, and she said we were the most
notorious bad children in town."

"She is the spitefullest woman they is,"
Jimmy's black eyes snapped; "she 'bout the
meddlesomest teacher in that school."

"Who telled you 'bout it, Lina?" questioned the other little girl.

"The Super'ntendent told his wife and
you know how some ladies are,— they just
can't keep a secret. Now it is just like
burying it to tell mother anything; she
never tells anybody but father, and grand-

mother, and grandfather, and Uncle Ed, and
Brother Johnson, and she makes them promise never to breathe it to a living soul. But
the Super'ntendent's wife is different; she
tells ever'thing she hears, and now everybody knows what that teacher said about
us."

"Everybody says she is the crankiest
teacher they is," cried Jimmy, "she won't
let you bring nothing to school 'cepting
your books; you can't even take your sling-
shot, nor your air-gun, nor ——"

"Nor your dolls," chimed in Frances, "and
she won't let you bat your eye, nor say a
word, nor cross your legs, nor blow your
nose."

"What do she think we 's goin' to her ol'
school fer if we can't have fun?" asked
Billy. "Tabernicle sho' had fun when he
went to school. He put a pin in the teacher's
chair an' she set down on it plumb up to
the head, an' he tie the strings together
what two nigger gals had they hair wropped
with, an' he squoze up a little boy's legs in
front of him with a rooster foot tell he
squalled out loud, an' he th'owed spitballs,
an' he make him some watermelon teeth,
an' he paint a chicken light red an' tuck it

to the teacher fer a dodo, an' he put cotton in his pants 'fore he got licked, an' he drawed the teacher on a slate. That 's what you go to school fer is to have fun, an' I sho' is goin' to have fun when I goes, an' I ain't goin' to take no bulldozin' offer her, neither."

"I bet we can squelch her," cried Frances, vindictively.

"Yes, we 'll show her a thing or two,"— for once Jimmy agreed with her, "she 'bout the butt-in-est old woman they is, and she 's going to find out we 'bout the squelchingest kids ever she tackle."

"Alfred Gage went to school to her last year," said Frances, "and he can read and write."

"Yes," joined in Jimmy, "and he 'bout the proudest boy they is; all time got to write his name all over everything."

"You 'member 'bout last Communion Sunday," went on the little girl, "when they hand roun' the little envellups and telled all the folks what was willing to give five dollars more on the pastor's sal'y just to write his name; so Alfred he so frisky 'cause he know how to write; so he tooken one of the little envellups and wroten 'Alfred Gage' on it; so when his papa find out 'bout it he say that kid got to work and pay that five dollars hi'self, 'cause he done sign his name to it."

"And if he ain't 'bout the sickest kid they is," declared Jimmy; "I'll betcher he won't get fresh no more soon. He telled me the other day he ain't had a drink of soda water this summer, 'cause every nickel he gets got to go to Mr. Pastor's sal'ry; he says he plumb tired supporting Brother Johnson and all his family; and, he say, every time he go up town he sees Johnny Johnson a-setting on a stool in Baltzer's drug store just a-swigging milk-shakes; he says he going to knock him off some day 'cause it's his nickels that kid 's a-spending."

There was a short silence, broken by Billy, who remarked, apropos of nothing:

"I sho' is glad I don't hafter be a 'oman when I puts on long pants, mens is heap mo' account."

"I wouldn't be a woman for nothing at all," Jimmy fully agreed with him; "they have the pokiest time they is."

"I 'm glad I am going to be a young lady when I grow up," Lina declared, "I would n't be a gentleman for anything.

I 'm going to wear pretty clothes and be beautiful and be a belle like mother was, and have lots of lovers kneel at my feet on one knee and play the guitar with the other ——"

"How they goin' to play the guîtar with they other knee?" asked the practical Billy.

"And sing 'Call Me Thine Own,'" she continued, ignoring his interruption. "Father got on his knees to mother thirty-seven-and-a-half times before she 'd say, 'I will.'"

"Look like he 'd 'a' wore his breeches out," said Billy.

"I don't want to be a lady," declared Frances; "they can't ever ride straddle nor climb a tree, and they got to squinch up their waists and toes. I wish I could kiss my elbow right now and turn to a boy."

CHAPTER XXVI

UNCONDITIONAL SURRENDER

THEY 'S going to be a big nigger 'scursion to Memphis at 'leven o'clock," said Jimmy as he met the other little boy at the dividing fence; "Sam Lamb 's going and 'most all the niggers they is. Sarah Jane 'lowed she 's going, but she ain't got nobody to 'tend to Bennie Dick. Would n't you like to go, Billy?"

"You can't go 'thout you 's a nigger," was the reply; "Sam Lamb say they ain't no white folks 'lowed on this train 'cepin' the engineer an' conductor."

"Sam Lamb 'd take care of us if we could go," continued Jimmy. "Let 's slip off and go down to the depot and see the niggers get on. There 'll be 'bout a million."

Billy's eyes sparkled with appreciation.

"I sho' wish I could," he said;" but Aunt Minerva 'd make me stay in bed a whole week if I went near the railroad."

"My mama 'd gimme 'bout a million licks, too, if I projeckted with a nigger 'scursion: she 'bout the spankingest woman they is. My papa put some burnt cork on his face in the Knights er Pythi's minstrels and I know where we can get some to make us black; you go get Miss Minerva's ink bottle too, that 'll help some, and get some matches, and I 'll go get the cork and we can go to Sarah Jane's house and make usselfs black."

"I ain't never promise not to black up and go down to the depot," said Billy waveringly. "I promise not to never be no mo' Injun — I ——"

"Well, run then," Jimmy interrupted impatiently. "We 'll just slip down to the railroad and take a look at the niggers. You don't hafto get on the train just 'cause you down to the depot."

So Miss Minerva's nephew, after tiptoeing into the house for her ink bottle and filling his pockets with contraband matches, met his chum at the cabin. There, under the critical survey of Bennie Dick from his customary place on the floor, they darkened their faces, heads, hands, feet, and legs; then, pulling their caps over their eyes, these energetic little boys stole out of the back gate and fairly flew down an alley to the station. No one noticed them in that hot, perspiring, black crowd. A lively band was playing and the mob of good-humored, happy negroes, dressed in their Sunday best, laughing and joking, pushing and elbowing,

made their way to the excursion train standing on the track.

The two excited children got directly behind a broad, pompous negro and slipped on the car just after him. Fortunately they found a seat in the rear of the coach and there they sat unobserved, still and quiet, except for an occasional delighted giggle, till the bell clanged and the train started off.

"We 'll see Sam Lamb toreckly," whispered Jimmy, "and he 'll take care of us."

The train was made up of seven coaches, which had been taking on negroes at every station up the road as far as Paducah, and it happened that the two little boys did not know a soul in their car.

But when they were nearing Woodstock, a little station not far from Memphis, Sam Lamb, making a tour of the cars, came into their coach and was promptly hailed by the children. When he recognized them, he burst into such a roar of laughter that it caused all the other passengers to turn around and look in their direction.

"What y' all gwine to do nex' I jes' wonder," he exclaimed. "Yo' ekals ain't made dis side o' 'ternity. Lordee, Lordee," he gazed at them admiringly, "you sho' is genoowine corn-fed, sterlin' silver, all-wool-an'-a-yard-wide, pure-leaf, Green-River Lollapaloosas. Does yo' folks know 'bout yer? Lordee! What I axin' sech a fool question fer? 'Course dey don't. Come on, I gwine to take y' all off 'm dese cars right here at dis Woodstock, an' we kin ketch de 'commodation back home."

"But Sam," protested Billy, "We don't want to go back home. We wants to go to Memphis."

"Hit don't matter what y' all wants," was the negro's reply, "y' all gotta git right off. Dis-here 'scursion train don't leave Memphis twell twelve o'clock to-night an' yuh see how slow she am runnin', and ev'y no 'count nigger on her 'll be full o' red eye. An' yo' folks is plumb 'stracted 'bout yer dis minute, I 'low. Come on. She am gittin' ready to stop."

He grabbed the blackened hand of each, pushing Jimmy and pulling Billy, and towed the reluctant little boys through the coach.

"Yuh sho' is sp'iled my fun," he growled as he hustled them across the platform to the waiting-room. "Dis-here 's de fus' 'scursion I been on widout Sukey a-taggin' long in five year an' I aimed fo' to roll 'em high; an' now, 'case o' ketchin' up wid y' all, I gotta go right back home. Now y' all set jes' as straight as yer kin set on dis here bench," he admonished, "whilst I send a telegraph to Marse Jeems Garner. An' don' yuh try to 'lope out on de flatform neider. Set whar I kin keep my eye skinned on yuh, yuh little slipp'ry-ellum eels. Den

I gwine to come back an' wash yer, so y' all look like 'spectable white folks."

Miss Minerva came out of her front door looking for Billy at the same time that Mrs. Garner appeared on her porch in search of Jimmy.

"William! You William!" called one woman.

"Jimmee-ee! O Jimmee-ee-ee!" called the other.

"Have you seen my nephew?" asked the one.

"No. Have you seen anything of Jimmy?" was the reply of the other.

"They were talking together at the fence about an hour ago," said Billy's aunt. "Possibly they are down at the livery stable with Sam Lamb; I 'll phone and find out."

"And I 'll ring up Mrs. Black and Mrs. Hamilton. They may have gone to see Lina or Frances."

In a short time both women appeared on their porches again:

"They have not been to the stable this morning," said Miss Minerva uneasily, "and Sam went to Memphis on the excursion train."

"And they are not with Lina or Frances,"— Mrs. Garner's face wore an anxious look, "I declare I never saw two such children. Still, I don't think we need worry as it is nearly dinner time, and they never miss their meals, you know."

But the noon hour came and with it no hungry little boys. Then, indeed, did the relatives of the children grow uneasy. The two telephones were kept busy, and Mr. Garner, with several other men on horseback, scoured the village. Not a soul had seen either child.

At three o'clock Miss Minerva, worn with anxiety and on the verge of a collapse, dropped into a chair on her veranda, her faithful Major by her side. He had come to offer help and sympathy as soon as he heard of her distress, and, finding her in such a softened, dependent, and receptive mood, the Major had remained to try to cheer her up.

Mr. and Mrs. Garner were also on the porch, discussing what further steps they could take.

"It is all the fault of that William of yours," snapped one little boy's mother to the other little boy's aunt: "Jimmy is the best child in the world when he is by himself, but he is easily led into mischief."

Miss Minerva's face blazed with indignation.

"William's fault indeed!" she answered back. "There never was a sweeter child than William;" for the lonely woman knew the truth at last. At the thought that her little nephew might be hurt, a long forgotten tenderness stirred her bosom and she realized for the first time how the child had grown into her life.

The telegram came.

"They are all right," shouted Mr. Garner joyously, as he quickly opened and read the yellow missive, "they went on the excursion and Sam Lamb is bringing them home on the accommodation."

As the Major, short, plump, rubicund, jolly, and Miss Minerva, tall, sallow, angular, solemn, were walking to the station to meet the train that was bringing home the runaways, the elderly lover knew himself to be at last master of the situation.

"The trouble with Billy ——" he began,

adjusting his steps to Miss Minerva's mincing walk.

"William," she corrected, faintly.

"The trouble with *Billy*," repeated her suitor firmly, "is this: you have tried to make a girl out of a healthy, high-spirited boy; you have n't given him the toys and playthings a boy should have; you have not even given the child common love and affection." He was letting himself go, for he knew that she needed the lecture, and, wonderful to tell, she was listening meekly. "You have steeled your heart," he went on, "against Billy and against me. You have about as much idea how to manage a boy as a — as a ——" he hesitated for a suitable comparison: he wanted to say "goat," but gallantry forbade; "as any other old maid," he blurted out, realizing as he did so that a woman had rather be called a goat than an old maid any time.

The color mounted to Miss Minerva's face.

"I don't have to be an old maid," she snapped spunkily.

"No; and you are not going to be one any longer," he answered with decision. "I tell you what, Miss Minerva, we are going to make a fine, manly boy out of that nephew of yours."

"We?" she echoed faintly.

"Yes, we! I said we, didn't I?" replied the Major ostentatiously. "The child shall have a pony to ride and every thing else that a boy ought to have. He is full of natural animal spirits and has to find some outlet for them; that is the reason he is always in mischief. Now, I think I understand children." He drew himself up proudly. "We shall be married to-morrow," he announced, "that I may assume at once my part of the responsibility of Billy's rearing."

Miss Minerva looked at him in fluttering consternation.

"Oh, no, not to-morrow," she protested; "possibly next year some time."

"To-morrow," reiterated the Major, his white moustache bristling with determination. Having at last asserted himself, he was enjoying the situation immensely and was not going to give way one inch.

"We will be married to-morrow and ——"

"Next month," she suggested timidly.

"To-morrow, I tell you!"

"Next week," she answered.

"To-morrow! To-morrow! To-morrow!" cried the Major, happy as a schoolboy.

"Next Sunday night after church," pleaded Miss Minerva.

"No, not next Sunday or Monday or Tuesday. We will be married to-morrow," declared the dictatorial Confederate veteran.

Billy's aunt succumbed.

"Oh, Joseph," she said with almost a simper, "you are so masterful."

"How would you like me for an uncle?"
Miss Minerva's affianced asked Billy a few
minutes later.

"Fine an' dandy," was the answer, as the
child wriggled himself out of his aunt's
embrace. The enthusiastic reception ac-
corded him, when he got off the train, was
almost too much for the little boy. He
gazed at the pair in embarrassment. He
was for the moment disconcerted and overcome; in place of the expected scoldings and
punishment, he was received with caresses
and flattering consideration. He could not
understand it at all.

The Major put a hand on the little boy's
shoulder and smiled a kindly smile into his
big, grey, astonished eyes as the happy lover
delightedly whispered, "Your aunt Minerva
is going to marry me to-morrow, Billy."

"Pants an' all?" asked William Green
Hill.

THE END

THE PUBLISHERS' STORY
of *Miss Minerva and*
William Green Hill

THOUSANDS OF MEN, women and children have read and enjoyed this unique little book, not only because of its infectious humor which brings a laugh with the reading of every page, but because Miss Minerva is a living expression of her type of womanhood, Billy a real, human, lovable little boy, and the other characters easily recognizable as those we meet every day.

It is not our purpose, though, to say much about a book that has become an intimate friend of so many, but rather to tell the story of its original publication, and something of its lamented author, Mrs. Calhoun.

Sometime during the spring of nineteen hundred and eight, a package came to us which contained, as was afterwards discovered, the manuscript of MISS MINERVA and WILLIAM GREEN HILL. In the course of busy preparation for the publications of the year, the modest package was laid aside and no attention given it until the receipt of the following rhymed letter on August twenty-second of that year:

> On the seventh of March, nineteen hundred and
>   eight,
> Mr. Reilly, I sent you my book,
> And sure since that date for a letter from you
> Each day I've continued to look.
>
> Is it pigeon-holed now where the bookworm alone
> May laugh and grow fat on each joke,
> Where canker and rust will eat out the hearts
> Of my dear little, quaint little folk?
>
> Or, alas, has it vanished from all human ken,
> The hard work of two long, long years?
> Will the public ne'er know of its merit and worth,
> Its laughter, its sighs and its tears?
>
> Or has it already been published in full,
> And the 'steenth printing given it fame?
> And instead of the title I gave it myself
> Is it christened with some other name?
>
> If naught has befallen it, may I still hope
> You'll send my lost child back to me?
> And I'll start it anew on its difficult path.
> Please ship it at once C. O. D.
>
>   FRANCES CALHOUN,
>   Covington, Tenn.

This unusual and politic appeal brought immediate action in our office, and Mr. Reilly unearthed the "treasure" of a manuscript and took it home. That evening he read it with surprise and delight; others who were given it to read were equally impressed, and this concurrence of favorable opinion led to the publication of the story February sixth, nineteen hundred and nine.

In response to a letter from us requesting of Mrs. Calhoun some facts concerning her life, and a photograph, we received on January twenty-second, nineteen hundred and nine, the following:

Covington, Tennessee. [Thursday.]

My dear Mr. Reilly:

I have not had my "tintype took" since I was a young girl—"several moons agone"—and I dislike very much the idea of having my printed likeness circulated around. However, I'll have some pictures made at once to send you.

My life has been so ordinary and commonplace that I don't think I have anything to relate that would interest the public. I used to help my father on his paper when he edited one here. I was a primary teacher in the Covington city school for seven years before I married. My husband died four years ago, just one year after our marriage.

My great grandfather Townes lived at Occoneechee, one of the famous old "before the war" country homes of southern Virginia.

I have had a few little verses printed in one of the Memphis dailies.

While eligible to join the Daughters of the American Revolution, I never have done so, preferring to give my time and attention to the Daughters of the Confederacy—of which organization I am a most enthusiastic member, being president of the local chapter. I am a Southerner of Southerners.

I am sorry I have not something more interesting to relate.

Sincerely yours,

FRANCES CALHOUN.

These were the only communications we had from Mrs. Calhoun. She never knew about the success, financial and artistic, achieved by her little book, nor anything of the thousands upon thousands who have tearfully laughed over the doings of the wonderful creatures of her imagination.

Frances Boyd was born in Mecklenburg County, Virginia, December twenty-fifth, eighteen hundred and sixty-seven, lived for about two years in Warrenton, North Carolina, and moved to Tennessee in eighteen hundred and eighty; graduated from the Tipton Female Seminary, Covington, Tennessee, in eighteen hundred and eighty-five, and married George Barret Calhoun in nineteen hundred and three. She died at her father's home in Covington, Tennessee, on June 8th, nineteen hundred and nine, but a few months after the publication of her book, and her body lies buried in the little cemetery there. This was her first and her only book, and it is a pity to think that her untimely death came just when she gave promise of adding so much to the store of human happiness.

THE PUBLISHERS.

THE UNIVERSITY OF TENNESSEE PRESS

KNOXVILLE 37916